PRAIRIE SCHOONER BOOK PRIZE IN FICTION

EDITOR: HILDA RAZ

DESTROY ALL

MONSTERS

{AND OTHER STORIES}

GREG HRBEK

UNIVERSITY OF NEBRASKA PRESS ∤ LINCOLN AND LONDON

Acknowledgments for the use of
copyrighted material appear on
page vii, which constitutes an
extension of the copyright page.

Library of Congress Cataloging-
in-Publication Data
Hrbek, Greg.
Destroy all monsters, and
other stories / Greg Hrbek.
p. cm. — (Prairie schooner
book prize in fiction)
ISBN 978-0-8032-3644-8
(pbk.: alk. paper)
I. Title.
PS3558.R47D47 2011
813'.54 — dc22
2011011197

Set in Chaparral by Bob Reitz.
Designed by Nathan Putens.

CONTENTS

ACKNOWLEDGMENTS

The following stories were previously published: "Sagittarius" in *Black Warrior Review* and *The Best American Short Stories 2009*; "Tomorrow People" in *Prairie Schooner*; "False Positive" in *Natural Bridge*; "Green World" in *Harper's Magazine*; "Destroy All Monsters" in *Conjunctions*; "Sleeper Wave" in *Sonora Review*; "The Cliffs at Marpi" in *The Bridport Prize 2006* (UK); "frannycam.net/diary" in *Salmagundi*; "General Grant (2004–)" in *The Idaho Review*; and "Bereavement" in *The 2007 Robert Olen Butler Prize Stories*.

DESTROY ALL MONSTERS

SAGITTARIUS

The land surrounding the house is state forest. A dirt road climbs farther up the mountain, where paint-stained bark indicates the direction of hiking trails and orange signs warn off hunters. It is into this wilderness that he has run away. Seven o'clock in the evening. While they were arguing (again) about the surgery, the baby vaulted over the rail of the playpen, as if it were a hurdle to be cleared. They heard his hooves scrabbling on the rubber mat but were too late to see him jump: tucking his forelegs up, hind legs flexing and thrusting, body tracing a parabola through the air; then the earthward reach of the forelegs, the tucking up of the rear hooves, the landing. They shouted his name in unison. When they reached the sunroom, they saw him bounding out the door. Upper half, human half, twisted in their direction; a look of joy and terror in the infant's eyes. But the equine part would not stop . . . Now he stands in the trees, hominid heart thundering in his chest. Though the twilight air is cold on the bare white skin of his torso, it can't touch him below the waist: his hindquarters are warm

under a coat of dark hair. He hears his mother call. "Sebastian!"
A flick of the tail, the shuffle of hooves. As he bounds deeper into
the maze of trees, night's first star appears in the ecliptic.

〉

The first fear blazing through her mind: someone with a rifle will
mistake him, in the mist of dawn, for an animal. No, Isabel thinks.
Dawn is ten hours away. We'll find him before then. We'll hear him
crying long before that. We have to. Hardly April. The temperature
still hypothermic at night. Even if he wanders for a mile, in this
silence we'll hear him. Except that his cries, until today, have
been so very faint . . . She herself can scarcely speak. When she
calls for him, his name seems to catch on spikes in her throat and
come out torn. She stops. Sweeps the flashlight through the trees.
Listens. All she hears is her husband's voice. Much stronger, more
certain than hers. Still, he sounds far away. Each time Martin calls
Sebastian's name, he sounds a little more distant; and Isabel feels
a little more alone in the dark. It seems very wrong to her, in these
moments, to be frightened for herself. But she is. A sense of the
future washes through her like the memory of a dream, vague and
unreliable but sharp nonetheless—an impression of a place she
will be one day. Dark, solitary, cut off from lovers and children.
She is thinking only of her baby. Where he is, how to reach him.
But every thought of him feels somehow like a thought about
herself. As if there's still a cord strung between them, a useless
cord that links them but doesn't keep them connected. She stops.
Listens. Sweeps the beam through the trees. There's a burning
in her chest as the light catches on two yellow eyes. Too big by
far, this animal. But in the moment before it bounds across the
road, darkness and hope conspire to let her see exactly what she
wants. For one blessed moment, it's him. Then it's a fawn darting
into the forest—with its mother chasing behind.

Martin could see, for a short time, the other beam sweeping up the dirt road and his wife's figure delineated in an auroral glow; but the space between them is widening—trees, darkness—and the light seems, from where he stands, to be going out. "Sebastian!" he shouts. He's careful to keep his voice free of anger so his son will not misinterpret his intentions. I don't want to punish you, I just want to help. He does not feel panicked. Worried, yes. Scared. But calm, clear enough to wonder if he might be succumbing to a state of shock. Probably he's been in shock for months already. He and Isabel both. Each in their own way. It's getting darker. Just since they've been out here (can't be more than four or five minutes), the sky has blackened enough to begin showing stars. The buds on the trees haven't opened yet, so the view to the firmament is clear. Martin only glances up; but that one glance is enough to remind him just how much space there is, in heaven and on earth, to get lost in. Again, he calls out. Hears only the clicking of crickets and the wind chime reverberations of traveling starlight. Then, noise from up the road, where he thinks his wife is.

"Is it him?" He waits for an answer. "Isabel?"

"A deer, I said."

She sounds shaken. Her voice already tinged with grief.

The boy sits on the couch watching the eyes of the cartoon characters bug out on the television and their tongues unfurl like party favors. Through the cotton of his pajamas, he tugs on his penis. He's three years old. He has never been alone in the house before. Although his parents sometimes threaten to leave him here (if he doesn't hurry up and get dressed or hurry up and get in the car), and though tears sometimes spring to his eyes at the thought, he always understands that the abandonment is not really going to occur. Yet here he is now. Left behind. At first, he was able to hear them calling his brother's name. Not anymore. He can't hear anything now. He has touched the remote control and made the voices on television go away. Now he can't hear anything but crickets marching closer and closer in the dark.

≀

Night is nearly done falling. Isabel thinks momentarily of Kaden, back at the house. She has never left him alone, unless you count the time she accidentally locked him inside with all the keys. After breaking in through the bedroom window, she found him sitting on the kitchen floor playing with the salad spinner. She thinks: he can take care of himself. Then her mind returns to the woods and her fears to wild animals. Raccoons, owls, black bear. What is her baby to these creatures? A peer, a brother—or an unknown encroacher? Isn't it all about territory, the cruel mathematics of the food chain? It occurs to her suddenly that this is all her fault. If she hadn't refused after the ultrasound to believe what the screen showed them; if she'd consented to the operation after the birth (at which point she could no longer deny the truth); and if she hadn't brought him out here, just today—only hours ago, they'd climbed this very road. If she hadn't shown him the world in all its openness and wildness. What happened today, what's happening even now: doesn't it validate the position she took from the very beginning? Her mind flashes back to the first appointment with the orthopedic surgeon. They hadn't even left the hospital yet. The baby was in neonatal intensive care; and there she was in that waiting room, with the magazines fanned out on the tables, those airbrushed cover photos, those mirages of flawlessness. Back in his office, the doctor told them their son would never walk. To increase the slim chances of ambulation, but mostly for the sake of anatomical correctness, he advised the removal of the two forelegs . . .

You mean amputate?

Mmm.

Is that . . . necessary?

Depends, Mrs. Avery, on your definition of necessity.

Martin leans against a tree and feels that some balance is tipping inside him. He closes his eyes, opens them again. Sees plainly, as if it's something caught in the beam of his flashlight, the futility of what they're trying to do. The baby could be anywhere! Abruptly, he starts back toward the house (remembering, all at once, his elder son). He intends to call the police, report a missing person. Then decides, with equal impulsiveness, against the idea. What kind of description would he give? How can he explain when he himself does not understand? Even the doctors can't make up their minds. The diagnosis changes every week. Spina bifida, muscular dystrophy, cerebral palsy as the cause of the musculoskeletal deformity; the body hair most likely the result of a condition called congenital hypertrichosis; and the extra legs—they don't have a clue. A genetic mutation, or the vestiges of a twin who failed to fully form. The fact is, no one knows exactly what's wrong with his son. No one knows what he is.

"Sebastian!"

His voice sounds, to his ears, less controlled this time. It's a fact that he, the father, is the cause of this situation. Had he responded differently back at the house, the baby would never have leapt over the rail of his playpen, knocked the back door open, and run away. A knife blade twists in his stomach. Suddenly, sharply, Martin is aware of his conduct. Out here, under the stars, he isn't sure if it made any sense at all . . . My son stood today. My son walked today.

Kaden walks down the hall, crying. Saying, "Where are you, Mom?" He knows they went out the back door. Still, he looks for them in the house. He goes to the bedroom first and speaks into the darkness. Gets no answer. He doesn't know where they've gone, yet their absence is part of a pattern. Kaden let his brother out the back door. His brother ran outside. His father ran through the door, his mother ran through the door. They have all disappeared into the night.

I let them out, he thinks.

Me.

I wanted to see my brother run. My brother is a horse.

❧

Isabel's foot slips. The ground is sloping upward. She realizes she's wearing sandals, and this pathetic detail pushes her to sob. She feels a surge of confusion. Not new. She's been feeling it—a dreamlike gap in logic, a page missing from the book—ever since the night he was born. There is a name for what he is. Why can't she think of it, why can't anyone think of it? After the delivery (which had been both easier and more difficult than Kaden's), she had not seen Sebastian right away. While she'd lain in the bed, her body light as a soul, a phalanx of nurses had spirited the newborn away. Nobody would answer her questions. Not the midwife. Not her own husband, who claimed to have seen nothing in the confusion. He sat beside her, worrying with his fingers the plastic wrist bracelet printed with his name and the name of their son. He took her hand, but wouldn't look at her. The lack of eye contact, though unnerving, allowed her to maintain a kind of distance. As if they were back in birthing class, watching a video about complications. As if the situation were purely hypothetical, a scenario invented for the purpose of instruction . . . Neonatal intensive care. First, a lobby with a nurses' station and a smaller room off to the side equipped with sinks. Isabel could not, for the life of her, figure out how to turn on the water. There were no handles on the faucet. She wondered then if she was dreaming, anaesthetized in the operating room; or still in the birthing suite, drugged even though she'd forsworn the drugs, and now she was hallucinating, succumbing to one of the adverse reactions that their birth-class instructor had warned them about: I can't breathe, I'm going into allergic shock, my heart is slowing, slowing, stopping. Suddenly, magically, water gushed from the faucet. Her husband's foot was depressing a pedal on the floor. Then they were going in. The unit was one large room, very quiet, full of incubators that made her think first of aquarium tanks, then display cases, then—because they were wheeled and curtained—of something else she couldn't quite put her finger on. The babies she could see were tiny, impossibly small, blue and mummified. Sebastian was not one of these. Not premature. Despite the debriefing with specialists, she didn't yet understand what he was. Was there no word for him, or simply no cute word, no word that didn't invoke a darker age? She was afraid, but relieved to feel, underneath the terror, crushed and barely breathing, but there, *there*, a desire to see him, a longing, whatever he might be. They neared his incubator. Positioned in a secluded corner of the room. The curtain was drawn. Monitors overhead displayed fluctuating numbers and jagged inscriptions. Under an impulse that upset her stomach and wrung her heart the way feelings of romance had when she was younger, Isabel moved closer. Yes, she had already fallen in love with him, with the idea of him. She'd made a space in her mind and heart, and now he would step into that shape and fit it perfectly, fill it perfectly. She reached out a hand and pulled open the curtain.

He thinks: my son walked today. Any other parent would be filled with a clear and simple happiness. For Martin, it is all too much. He had come home half an hour ago, with a bottle of red wine and the honest intention to start from scratch. No made-up minds, no sides. They would talk, really talk. Work things out together. Figure out what to do. Then he walked in the door and his older son grabbed him by the hand and pulled him back into the sunroom where his wife was waiting and beaming with joy; and then he saw the reason—the baby was standing, standing on all four feet—and he couldn't understand why, but his spirits simply collapsed, and all his hopes seemed like a fantasy compared to the concrete fact of the creature in the playpen.

He's standing, Dad.

I can see that.

Not only that, said his wife. He can walk. He got up in the meadow today, on the grass, and walked.

Like a foh-wul, Kaden said.

A what?

Dad, a foh-wul is a baby horse.

He's not a foal.

Isabel continued: He fell down at first. But then he did it, Martin, just like they said he wouldn't.

Martin looked again. No illusion. Surrounded by the trappings of any boy's infancy—a floppy blue teddy bear; a plush baseball with a jingle bell inside; a mobile of the solar system, its planets swaying in a lazy orbit—their disabled son was standing. Eyes wide, hands clapping, he bounced on his four legs, hooves scrabbling on the polyester mat. Martin walked over to him and placed a hand on his head, and said, We can't let him do this.

Why not?

He'll get used to it.

She smiled uncertainly. I don't see what you mean, she said.

Yes, you do.

I don't actually.

He'll get used to standing like this. We won't be able to break him of the habit.

Standing isn't a habit.

Okay.

Nose picking is a habit. Thumb sucking, she said, tears coming into her eyes. Christ, even today? Even this? I don't understand you.

No kidding.

How can this be anything but wonderful?

It's only going to make everything harder. The longer we wait, the harder it's going to be. For all of us.

He slipped past her, taking pains to avoid brushing any part of his body against hers. She followed him down the hallway to the stairs. Leaving the two children behind.

You just wish he'd go away, she said too loudly.

Untrue.

Not just half of him. All of him.

Kaden remembers the back door. Wonders what he's doing here, at home, when the rest of them have run away. Back in the sunroom, he stares at the empty playpen. The mobile of the solar system hangs frozen in the darkness. His brother had set it whirling when he jumped. Jump, Kaden had whispered. Down the hall, they'd been saying, Go away. All of him. Kaden opened the back door. Go, brother. Now the boy feels a heat, like a candle burning in his belly. He feels for his sneakers in the pile of shoes beside the door. Pulls them on the wrong feet. Steps into the starry night and onto the road.

◊

Suddenly, she thinks, The meadow! Of course. That's where he went. Is now. A realization so sharp, so visual—she can *see* him, a four-legged shadow tracing a lazy path through the grass—as to make her feel clairvoyant. Isabel starts to reach for her cell phone, to speed-dial her husband and tell him where to meet her: she's confident enough now in a happy ending to laugh at the impulse. She runs back down the road. Seeking out the trailhead with the flashlight beam. The memory of the afternoon speeding a dizzy spin in her head.

She hadn't been sure, earlier in the day, if the ground of the meadow would be dry (the last of the snow had melted only recently), yet the world wore the beckoning look of spring. She packed a blanket in the backpack and managed to get him into the front pouch, his forelegs through the two extra holes she'd cut in the padding. All through the winter, Sebastian had confirmed his doctors' expectations — sleeping excessively, communicating only through weak cries, showing little interest in his surroundings — but now, in the outdoors, he observed everything with wide eyes and squawked like a tropical bird. How beautiful to hear! Isabel felt a strength bubble up from deep inside her. We can get through this, she thought. All of us together. As she carried him through the woods, she felt strangely blessed. As if this improbable child, as he appeared right now, was the fulfillment of some secret wish. They found the meadow golden with sun. The flaxen grass long and dry enough. Isabel freed the baby from the carrier, laid him down on the blanket. Immediately he started struggling. A seizure, an allergic reaction? She was about to sweep him up again and rush down the trail, back to the house and the telephone, when she realized there was something methodical, something conscious about his movements. The knobby, hairy legs stretched and slipped, stretched and slipped. Then the bones momentarily straightened and locked, and his body almost lifted from the ground. He tried again. Again and again. To hoist himself up. To balance. The closer he got, the more violently his legs trembled. So frail, she thought. Like they might snap under his weight. Scary; but she gently urged him on, supporting his underbelly with a hand. She shaking too—and feeling, too, that she was rising somehow. It took an hour, maybe more; yet the day was far from over, the sun still warm and high overhead when she heard herself say, in a broken whisper, Look at you, little man. Look at you standing up.

Now, searching for the trailhead, she again feels weightless with thanks. Yes, everything's going to be alright. She calls out to her husband. "Martin! Can you hear me?" But a vehicle, a pickup truck, is coming down the mountain, tires rasping against the dirt road, columns of halogen light careering through the trees and blinding her as she moves out of the way.

Martin can barely admit it to himself, but his wife is right. He does sometimes wish the baby would disappear. Not half of him. All of him. Now it's happening. And if they don't find him—if they do and it's too late . . . His mind projects a scene: his return to the house in the gray light of dawn, exhausted and empty-handed. It comes to him like a psychic flash, crisp and definite, this picture of himself. Followed by another that's simply unbearable: their second child dead on a carpet of last autumn's rust-colored leaves. Not the first time he has imagined such a thing. Ever since the doctors started talking about life expectancy, Martin has been fighting off dark imagery. We can't be sure (they say), we need more neuromotor assessment, and intelligence tests are a year away, but physical deformities this severe suggest associated malformations of the brain; and if the muscle disease is degenerative, as it almost certainly is—well, it's only a matter of time before it reaches the heart, which is, in the end, just another muscle . . . What would be worse? Losing the boy tonight (just a baby, five months in the world and already gone from it) or losing him thirteen years from now? No, he doesn't want his son to vanish. He just wants him to be normal. He wants fatherhood to be free of pain and paradox.

Suddenly, his hands are breaking a fall. Fucking rock, fucking root of a tree. He hits the ground, pant leg tearing on something. Kneeling now on the forest floor, ankle possibly sprained, he becomes aware of an open space ahead. Dark, but lighter than the woods.

The meadow.

For a moment, the father can hear something in the grass. A tiny voice. Musical and human. Very small, very clear. There—then gone. Cancelled by the sound of a car or truck bounding down the mountain road.

Kaden feels his way along the road. For a few yards, before the trees get thick, the night is like a picture in a storybook: the road faintly glows, but on every page it gets a little blacker. The boy stops, looks back. Focuses on a window of the house pulsing with television light. Figures out, finally, why his feet are hurting. He sits on the rocky dirt. Taking sneakers off is one thing; trying to put them back on in the dark is another. He remembers one time in the car (he had no brother yet and his seat faced backward) seeing through the window a girl with dark glasses and a long silver wand that showed her where to go. He needs a wand. Without a wand, he will never, ever find them. He holds a sneaker up to the sky, eyes squinting and blinking. Slowly, the object comes clear to him. The red stripes, the contour of the toe. Not until the light grows bright enough to reveal the terrain of the road and to make the trunks of trees leap out from the forest does Kaden wonder about the source of it, turning his head, imagining that such radiance could only come from a friendly, enchanted star.

ᘏ

She glimpses the trailhead (the little tin marker, stick figure with walking stick, nailed to the tree) and hears, at the very same moment, the panic of wheels going into a skid, treads clawing violently at dirt and rock, then the collision—crush of metal, bleat of a horn—and the harmonics of breaking glass. Isabel freezes. Same as when she wakes in her bed, having heard something that may have been nothing. Running down the road now is like all the times she has moved through her home in the dead of night. This is something, this is nothing . . . Isn't that also what she told herself in the days after the ultrasound? On that screen, they had seen the ghost of an impossible fetus. Six limbs. Two arms and four legs, each foot badly twisted and missing toes. She saw the images with her own eyes (the technician had printed enough pictures to fill a scrapbook). She heard everything the doctors said in the days afterward about how and why and what to do about it. Still, a patchy fog obscured her vision. Static broke on her eardrums like ocean waves. A few months later she reached for that curtain in the NICU, fearing suddenly that she might be about to suffer a crippling blow. But no. As she pulled the curtain aside, her body felt no shock from without, only a sweet confirmation from within. Not like other boys. And not entirely human. But why all this grave talk of abnormalities and deformities, when anyone can see he is exquisitely formed? A beautiful boy from the waist up, and from the waist down, a beautiful horse . . . Now she runs, as on a tightrope. Each time she blinks, a film of tears spreads evenly over the surface of her eyes, and through this aqueous medium, the light down below (dim; one headlight bulb must have burst on impact) looks like an aura suffusing the scene of the accident. No, no, no. A voice in her head, hers but not hers, keeps saying the word, as if refusing to find something horrible is to omit it from reality. When she reaches the foot of the hill, feet skidding, her lungs crumple and contract. No room for air. The truck is sunk front-first in a ditch at a forty-five-degree angle, rear wheels in the air, hood reshaped by a tree trunk. The driver, ejected from his seat and halfway through the windshield—lower body in the cab, upper on the glass-spangled hood—isn't moving. "Oh God," the mother says aloud. Then starts calling for her baby. Shining the light into the ditch; into the trees; finally onto the road, where it finds first a tiny red-striped sneaker, then her other son, her human son, sitting in the dirt, staring, mesmerized by the wreck.

Though Martin hears the crash, he is also deaf to it. In the peace that follows, there seems to be only one sound in the universe: it comes from the heart of the meadow. "Uh-boo-boo-bah. Uh-voo. Uh-bah-bah-bah-bah-bah." Martin can see him—a four-legged shadow moving through the grass—and as the father emerges from the trees, the sky above the child expands. Not the first time he's been out here after dark. Last summer he made love with his wife under this blown-glass sky. Still, the place feels like a new discovery to him. Never has he seen a thicker spread of stars. Beneath all those dots of light, the baby continues to murmur in a private dialect. When Martin comes within a few yards, he stops and whispers:

"Sebastian."

The boy turns—neither startles and runs off, nor comes rushing into his daddy's arms. It's as if the parent has been present all along, as if there's nothing extraordinary about the situation. Again, he thinks, My son is walking. Only this time, the idea, the sight of it, gives him a shiver of amazement. He crouches down and watches. He watches his strange son walk. Emotion twists once more like a knife in his belly. If up to Martin alone, the surgery would have been performed long ago. The forelegs lopped off. After that, an operation to alter the angle of the femur and another (involving the imbedding of metal hooks and wires) to straighten the spine. Six weeks in a cast. Then laser hair removal. Genital reconstruction. The doctors call it medical necessity. He can't stay like this. He will never walk. He never will—But he is. Ever since the birth, Martin has been praying he'll wake up. Wake up to find that the world is really a mundane place. Now, under the zodiac sky with this infant, he sees the absurdity of the notion; and with a trembling inside, he thinks to turn away from it. The insight seems part of the night, part winter and part spring, something he can breathe in and keep breathing in. Very slowly, he stands and moves closer. Places a hand on the boy's body, on his bare back, the root of his spine, where soft white skin grades into a coat of hair.

ך

He will fall asleep now: here, in his father's arms, long before they reach the house, before they come upon the accident. Breathing the sweet fumes of pine needles. Feeling through the father's flesh the warmth of flowing blood, which is his blood too. When Martin starts to run, Sebastian's eyes will flutter open. He will glimpse the light, the vehicle, the body slumped over the hood. But he won't remember. He won't remember and he'll never forget the night he ran away and his father brought him home. It's the kind of impossible story that holds a family together. You tell it over and over again; and with the passage of time, the tale becomes more unbelievable and at the same time increasingly difficult to disprove, a myth about the life you carry.

TOMORROW PEOPLE

The year they took San Francisco and my sister forever away, I was still a baby. But in 2038, I was eleven years old, going on twelve.

My family lived, in those days, on a cul-de-sac named after an extinguished tribe of Native Americans, in a house nearly a century old, a split-level ranch from the days of roof antennas. Next door, in a house of nearly identical size and design, lived my best friend since kindergarten, a boy who'd learned in the course of our fifth-grade genealogy project that there'd been a lynching in his family tree. In tribute to that great-uncle, my friend had changed his name to Zebedee. Only I still called him Plaxico. Of the twelve families in our subdivision, five (including Plaxico's) were black; seven (counting mine), white. It was an aberration of racial demographics that, since I had moved there, eight years earlier, we'd had no brown-skinned neighbors—until Abdelkarim Hussein Mohamed al-Nasr became the son and heir of Franklin D. Banfelder, a widower who every summer would bestow ice pops upon the children of the neighborhood, the same way he'd bestowed chocolate, back in his days as a contract soldier, upon the children of the faraway homeland of Abdelkarim.

❡

Mr. Banfelder had left town a week after school's end, not telling anyone where he was going. No sooner did he disappear than the periodical cicadas tunneled out of their underground cells for the first time since the year 2021. One evening around sunset, we heard a whisper everywhere. The nymphs were coming out. Shuffling by the millions to the trunks of trees and crawling up to the leafy branches. They made no sound that night. By the next morning, they had started to molt. I discovered one in my window, bonded to the fine wires of the screen. The insect wasn't free of itself yet. The nymphal body had dehisced down the back, a divide so clean it looked like the work of a surgeon; and the new body, white and waxen, was humping through the cleft. After the back, the head began to break open—the eyes diverged and new eyes came into view, looking directly into mine.

By the time Mr. Banfelder's microcompact reappeared, our world was dizzy with their noise. We'd heard a rumor. Mr. B had gone to Iraq. Gone by himself, but come back with a kid. My friends and I rode over there, the tires of our bikes crushing a crust of shed exoskeletons; and when Mr. B answered the doorbell and saw the four of us on the porch, he got a look on his face like he'd been waiting all morning and said, "Boys, there's someone I want you to meet. Dorian, Dean, Zeb, Damian . . . This is Abdelkarim."

And there he was.

The kid who was like us except he wasn't, because his skin wasn't white and it wasn't black. (It was, I would later determine, the shade of the crayon in my box called "tumbleweed.")

"Does he speak English?" Dean asked.

"Ask him," said Mr. B, lighting up a green. "He doesn't bite."

"Okay. Do you speak English?"

"Qalilan," the kid said.

"That means 'a little bit' in Arabic." Then Mr. Banfelder spoke to the boy in his native tongue and, nodding encouragingly, pointed to the four of us.

Finally, the kid said: "I pledge allegiance . . . to the flag . . . of . . ."

"Of . . . the United States . . ."

"United States . . ."

"Of . . ."

"Of . . ."

"America."

"Amereeka."

I wondered if they were going to recite the whole thing word by word, then maybe sing the national anthem. But Mr. Banfelder just nodded, as if very proud of the boy's effort. At long last, he said, "Ice pops, anyone?"

We followed him into the kitchen, where there were now five chairs around the glass table instead of the usual four.

"Take a load off," said Mr. B. "How have you boys been? I leave for a week and return to find a plague being visited. What the hell'd you do while I was gone, huh?"

He opened the freezer and removed the box of ice pops, the same kind he'd been buying and supplying us with for years. Never cream pops, never fudge pops. Only ice pops. No flavor requests. We took what we got and we liked it. We came for the treat and stayed for stories about the war.

"Is he from . . . over there?" I asked.

"Najaf," said Mr. B.

Abdelkarim looked up at the sound of this familiar word. Mr. B said something in Arabic and the kid blinked his huge dark eyes, and then Mr. B explained to us that the kid didn't have any parents, didn't have any family at all, because they'd all been killed when a laser-guided bomb, which was supposed to land on the house of a known insurgent, fell through the roof of an unknown family of oil workers.

"I gotta get home," Damian said.

"Me, too," said Dean.

"Suck and run, is that it?" It sounded like his feelings were hurt. "Hey, I'm just kidding. You guys do your thing. We'll see you around." Then he turned to Abdelkarim and said something like he was trying to get *him* to say something. But Abdelkarim didn't say anything else that day. From below a hurricane of black hair and angry accent mark eyebrows, he seemed to be looking into our minds and reading them while a grape ice pop turned his lips cadaver purple.

"Plan for the future," my brother said that night. "That Ay-rab is here to stay." Our parents had fallen asleep in front of the television, and the two of us had retired to the screened-in gazebo in the backyard, which my big brother had been referring to, ever since he'd registered for the draft, as the Veterans of Unjust Wars Hall. Cliff was eighteen then: nearly twice as old as me; twice as tall; two times more likely to make a joke about something that wasn't the least bit funny.

"Staying? Why?"

"Because he's Abdelkarim Banfelder now."

The butane lighter scritched; a tiny flame genuflecting as my brother inhaled and the bong water gurgled.

"I don't like him," I finally said.

"Because he's an Ay-rab?"

"No."

"Dorian," my brother said, "don't be such a dead white male."

What was he talking about? Everyone who'd gone over there and not come back, gone and come back with a flag draped over their casket? Despite the heat of the night, the idea made me cold.

"What'll you do?" I asked.

"If what?"

"If, you know."

We had not discussed, neither the two of us in private nor the family as a unit, the prospect of his going to war.

I had been surprised on his eighteenth birthday when he'd obeyed the law, because he had always been against it all. In high school, my brother had spent his afternoons neither wandering aimlessly through the mall nor challenging gravity at the skate park, but ensconced behind the walls of Café Pravda. In that place where the art exhibit never changed, kids who plumed their hair like rock stars from my father's old record collection would hype themselves up on energy drinks and plan acts of civil disobedience.

"You know Plaxico," I said.

"Mmm."

"You know his brother, Miles."

"The oboe player."

"He's going into hiding," I said. "In Canada."

"That's original."

Through the trees shone the moon, casting enough light to make me feel we were actors playing ourselves in a very old movie. I finally said: "Maybe you could go with him." Again, my brother set the brick of opium burning; the foul water glugged. Smoke in the bong: a trapped djinn my brother took into his lungs and held there before releasing it into the motionless air of the gazebo, where it hovered as if waiting to grant our wishes.

Cliff wasn't my only sibling. I had an older sister, too. Or I'd had one once; at least, I thought I'd had one—an older sister who had died eight years earlier, when an improvised nuclear device had been exploded in the city where she'd just started college.

She had been seventeen (Cliff ten, I three) when she literally disappeared without a trace. A lot of victims of that attack—their bodies, their bones and teeth—were never found. This was different. Along with her physical self, every artifact of my sister had vanished. For example, we had no pictures. My parents, I believed, had expunged from the family albums every image of her. Her bedroom? There was none, because we'd moved clear across the country after that impossible day. Childhood toys, school notebooks, old clothes. Given away or buried in a landfill or burned to ash. I dreamed of her. Of a girl with long dark hair and eyes the green of leaves about to change color, whose rounded cheekbones and cleft chin reminded me of my own mirror image. In the dreams, we were always in the city of her death. I had never been there but had spent hours clicking on the hundreds of thousands of archived images. Most terrible to me (even more than the video footage of the blast recorded by phones and weather cameras) were the before-and-after pictures of that place: iconic buildings stripped to architectural bone; the great bridge deleted, save for one carbonized pillar . . .

One morning over breakfast, alone with my mother, I said something about it. I waited, like a hunter hiding in a blind, until she had sat down with me and had stirred some fake sugar into her coffee; and as she was raising the cup to her lips, I said: "I had a dream about her." I was watching for a sign. Some reflex. A tremor in the hand, a contraction of the pupils. She didn't even blink. "A dream about who, sweetie?"

❧

The morning after we met him, my phone rang. Damian. His picture ID was a cartoon naked lady with a whip. "Don't go to your snailbox," he commanded.

"Why not?"

"The towelhead just put something in it."

"So?"

"So anthrax," he said.

I hung up on him and went out to investigate. Barely nine o'clock and the air was already hot. We had an oak tree in our front yard, a hundred years old, a hundred feet tall. Trembling from the trunk to the high branches with veiny-winged insects whose trilling seemed to get louder the nearer my body came to the mailbox.

Inside: a small, square envelope. Bright blue. My name printed carefully in a schoolboy's hand. I unstuck the flap. No deadly poof of dust. Just a card featuring a happy killer whale doing a backflip.

My phone rang.

"There's some weird white powder in here," I said.

"Just what is it, asshole? What's the little suicide bomber up to?"

"It's an invitation. To a pool party."

My friend didn't say anything. I ripped the card and envelope in half. "Fuggin' unbelievable," Damian finally said. "I mean, Jesus Jones. Like we're gonna go play Marco Polo with Jig-Abdul of Arabia."

That night at family dinner, my mother—a New Liberal who had been telling me and my brother ever since we could sit in a highchair that, as a teenager voting for the first time, she had helped elect a black president—said she'd heard about the pool party and thought it was incredibly brave for a boy in his situation to put himself out there like that.

"What's his name, Dorian?"

"Dunno."

"His name," Cliff said, "is Abdelkarim Hussein Mohamed al-Nasr Banfelder. But you can call him Camel Fucker for short."

"Cliff," my father said.

We had a rule about racial slurs in our house. If I had said it, there would've been consequences. I stared at the stuffed green pepper on my plate.

"Abdelkarim," my mother said. "I wonder if he's Sunni or Shia."

"He's from Najaf," Cliff said.

"Shia," my father said. "More likely than not."

My brother seemed skeptical. "Well, whatever his denomination, it should be a blast. Nothing like a pool party, right, pal o' mine?"

"Mm," I said.

"Do some cannonballs, drink some punch, jam to some Arab death metal."

"Is there a problem with your pepper?" my father asked me.

"It looks like a dead frog."

"Have to agree, Dad. Ixnay on the epperpay." Despite the negative review, Cliff served himself another, cut along the midline of the vegetable, scooped out the organs. "You *are* gonna go, right?" He was talking to me now.

"Go where?"

"To Abdelkarim's party."

"Of course he's going," my mom said.

I just sat there, while beyond the bay window the sun capsized in a sea of tropospheric aerosols. They say that airborne pollutants robbed intensity from the sunsets of our childhood; but in my recollection, every afternoon ended with the colors of holocaust, and you took a moment, while the sky was on fire, to remember the people who'd been spirited away.

"I don't like pool parties," I finally said.

My mother gave me a hard stare. "Since when? Since when do you not like pool parties?"

"Yeah," Cliff said, "since when, xenophobe?"

"I'm not a xenophobe."

"Then why," my mother said. "Last summer you went to pool parties."

"I'm going into sixth grade now."

"Dorian, we're not going to let this kind of thing slide. Every time something comes up—"

"Not every—"

She stopped me with a traffic-cop gesture. She seemed to be turning a seasick green, like the sky over the plains before the clouds twist. We all knew what my mother was going to dredge up: the mosque. All the sudden, my eyes were burning on the inside.

"I don't have to remind you," she said.

"No."

"So, in other words, you'll call them after dinner and tell them thanks, you can't wait, and then you'll go over there on Saturday and make the boy feel welcome and maybe try to find some space in your heart for someone who's lost everything—everything, Dorian—and who could really use some friends right now."

It was about five months earlier that Ms. Morano, our Social Studies teacher, had announced a field trip to the nearest Islamic center.

I didn't want to go.

What I wanted was for my parents to not sign the consent form. I knew that Damian's wouldn't. I figured half the class wouldn't be going. "Then you'll be in the open-minded half," my mother said, scribbling her signature . . .

In the end, twelve of twenty got on the bus and hadjed into the state capital, which on sunny hot days appeared from the northway exit as a scale model of itself enclosed in a transparent sphere aswirl with photochemical smog. My class had been here before. The state museum was here: a windowless maze of passages and galleries filled with everything from giant, century-old combustion-engine automobiles to the mounted bodies of extinct birds whose archived souls called out from speakers in the ceiling. My mother worked in this city. There was an airport; a river from which tour boats emerged like tetrapods, to climb over land to the houses of government; and a mosque with a tit-like dome and two minarets that looked exactly like a couple of intercontinental ballistic missiles.

I remember feeling a knot of emotions—mostly anger and nervousness—as we pulled into the parking lot and disembarked from the bus and walked toward the main entrance, where the imam awaited us in his long white robe. I was not angry at the imam. He wasn't very tall and his voice was soft and his skin was black. As he led us through the place, showing us all the things we'd read about in our textbook (the wall that faced Mecca and the mimbar from which the khatib delivered the khutbah), I thought about how most Muslims in America were like him, and how most of the people who came to worship here were probably like him, and how I had nothing against people like him. Despite all that, in the bathroom (in a stall that looked exactly like every other stall in the world, containing a toilet that looked like every other toilet), I unzipped my backpack and removed the Magic Marker and wrote on the metal partition: TERRORISTS GO HOME.

And I did call over there that night, from a chair in the family room while my mother stood five feet away violating my communicational privacy.

"Hello?"

"Mr. B. Hi. It's me, Dorian Wakefield."

"Mr. D," he said.

"I'm just calling to say I'll be at the party on Saturday. I can't wait."

"That's great. Abdelkarim will be very happy to hear that. Look, why don't you tell him yourself. He's right here."

Silence on the line. Tell him myself? Tell him how? Still, my mother stood there. I could hear Mr. Banfelder talking to Abdelkarim in Arabic. It went on for a while, and I started to get the gist of it. The kid didn't want the phone. Finally, I could hear some breathing. Then a meek "Marhaban."

"That means 'hello,'" Mr. Banfelder said. "I'm on in the other room here. I'll interpret—you guys make like a couple of world leaders. Go ahead, Mr. Ambassador."

"Me? Okay, um. Hello."

"Marhaban."

"Mar-ban," I said, and Mr. B told me I didn't have to repeat what *he* said; he would merely be saying in Arabic whatever I had already said in English, so I should just say whatever I wanted and vice versa for Abdelkarim. My mother had cocked her head curiously. I felt like I was going to cry.

"Okay, I . . ."

Some empathetic angel must have come down and shooed my mother away, because she crossed her arms, did a graceful about-face, and left me alone. After which I said to Abdelkarim that I would be coming to the party. And Mr. Banfelder said that in Arabic. And Abdelkarim said something that translated as, Good, I am happy about that. But he didn't sound happy about it. He sounded about as happy as *I* was about the whole thing. There was an awkward silence now. I could hear my mother in the kitchen, loading the dishwasher. I tried to think of what to say. *Have you ever played a video game? Where were you when the bomb fell through the roof?* Suddenly, the power went out. The lights snapped off; the air conditioners fell silent; the overhead paddle fans completed a few last lazy revolutions.

"Shit," said Mr. B.

"Biraz," said Abdelkarim.

"That means 'shit,'" Mr. B explained. Then he said something to his son that sounded like the basic hypocritical dad reprimand except with a lot more epiglottal stress. "The mouth on this kid," he said. "Well, here we all are again. In the dark."

Abdelkarim said something that translated as, I have to urinate. Mr. B told him to say something, and Abdelkarim said: "Ma'salama."

"That means 'goodbye.'"

"Bye," I said.

"Ma'salama," said Mr. B.

I knew he wasn't saying ma'salama to me, just telling Abdelkarim in Arabic that I had said goodbye in English. So I didn't hang up. And neither did he. Before that night, I had never talked on the phone to Mr. Banfelder. I had been in his house a million times—even in the basement, where he kept the memorabilia from his days in the Middle East. I'd seen a framed photograph of one of his teams (standing around a sport-utility vehicle with a turret gun on the roof) and another with just him and an American diplomat whose life he'd saved in Baghdad. I'd read his letter of commendation from the White House. And I'd taken a turn holding in my hands his old Glock nine-millimeter pistol. Now I felt uneasy. As if only now, on the phone, connected in a darkness by nothing but electromagnetic waves, could I see that he really was a stranger to me.

"Dorian," he finally said, "you're a good goddamn kid."

"Thanks."

"Ma'salama," he said; and though I knew he expected me to respond in kind, I couldn't bring myself to say the word.

In my dreams, we were always in the city of her death. Walking together through the wasteland; or running through it, fleeing something. Or I'd be alone, searching for her. Once, I found her in a tiny room inside the coastal windmill, sitting at a spinning wheel, weeping; another time, in the middle of an empty street, I stepped on her fossilized remains. I can't remember which dreams happened on which nights—except for a few, whose images and storylines would've never been born if not for the events of a specific day. That night, I was up on the top of the headlands and the great bridge was still there, joining the headlands to the city, and the city was there, gleaming on the other side of the bridge as in the pictures taken before.

I had the invitation to the party.

Not with me; I had hidden it somewhere, as if it was something I wanted to keep. I was hiding it from her. Then suddenly we were standing on the bridge together—only there was no bridge anymore . . .

If I cried out in my sleep that night, no one heard over the white noise of the air-conditioning. "Time," I said. "Twelve thirty-five, a.m.," my phone responded. Maybe my father would still be awake. I got out of bed and switched on a light and pulled on some pajama bottoms. Sure enough, noise in the den. Fingers clip-clopping on a keyboard. I went down the stairs and stood in the doorway. As usual, my father was seated on the couch, hunched over his ancient notebook computer. The only light in the room came from the candescent screen. He stopped typing. Looked in my direction. Took the canalphones out of his ears. I sat down and let him fold an arm around me. While weird music leaked from the elastomer plugs, he held me but didn't ask what was wrong. Finally, the computer went to sleep and started dreaming a slideshow of family photos.

"California," I said.

"Mm hm."

"You look so young," I said.

"I *was* so young."

The picture (one it seemed I'd never seen before) had faded, replaced by another much more recent, but my mind's eye had saved the image: a close-up of my parents on the sand, chins resting on their hands, my mother wearing huge sunglasses that looked like outmoded virtual reality goggles, both of them truly smiling while a blue ocean wave crested in the background.

"What year was that?"

"On the beach? '20. Maybe '21."

"So Cliff was just a baby."

"More or less," my father said. "Of course, Cliff still *is* a baby, more or less."

"Who took the picture?"

My father didn't say anything. I thought to myself: she would've been six or seven. The photos continued to appear and disappear.

"Dad . . ."

"The one on the beach?" He breathed and seemed to keep the air inside for longer than normal. Then he said he really couldn't remember. Maybe they'd been with friends. Maybe the Magic Paparazzi took it.

"I'm too old for that joke," I said.

"Okay."

"It wasn't the timer. You can tell from the angle. Someone was lying down in front of you."

He squinted at me, as if he couldn't see what there was to be upset about. Then the expression on his face changed. "Look, Dorian. If you want my honest opinion, I think your mother was a little hard on you last night."

I watched the pictures of us come and go.

"The thing is," he went on, "she's basically right. We need to live with people. Not just tolerate them. Be friends with them, go to their parties once in a while. You know what Lincoln said about the better angels of our nature. This is just one of those times when you have to be the better angel."

I said I didn't know anything about Abraham Lincoln.

"Sure, you do."

"No, I don't."

"I'll bet you a frozen custard you know three things about him."

I thought to myself: she would've been six or seven, lying in the sand right in front of them. Holding the camera very close to them. My father on the left; my mother on the right. Suddenly, it occurred to me: the big lenses of the sunglasses . . . she might be reflected in them. I could open the file in the photo editor and magnify it . . .

"Well," my father said, "you sleep on it." He released me from his embrace and leaned forward and waved his finger over the touch pad.

"Wait, I want to see that picture."

"What picture?"

"Of you on the beach."

He told me there were a million photos on the hard drive. When I asked him to do a search, he said he couldn't remember what he'd named it (or if he ever *had* named it) and he wasn't about to start looking for it now. When I said I would look for it, he said he was writing. When I told him I would go get one of my flash drives, he gave me that squinty look again.

"You want me to copy you all those pictures? I don't know. There are a lot of old pictures in there."

"So?"

"So maybe there are some I don't want you to see."

"Of what?" I said. "Of who?"

"Of *who*? Of your mother. And that's not a dis, there really might be naked pictures of her in there. From back in the day."

I just looked at him.

"Fine," he finally said. "If it's so important, I'll give you a copy." He picked up the canalphones and plugged up his ears. "Tomorrow."

❡

Damian gave Mr. B some bullshit about his grandmother fracturing her femur in a home for the memory impaired. Dean had a steel drum lesson. Come Saturday, it was just me and Plaxico in our cargo trunks and sun-protective shirts and flip-flops heading up the curve of the cul-de-sac to the party. If you could call this a party: three kids, one of whom spoke no English, and a seventy-year-old former soldier of fortune. But then an unfamiliar car rolled by us. Two kids in the back. It was heading for Mr. B's driveway, where another alien vehicle was already parked. A woman in a head scarf stood by the open driver's door. A kid was walking from that car to the house. Dressed just like us. Dressed for swimming. I stopped there, at the outskirts of the neighboring lawn, which belonged to the Nkondos, whose son, Ryder, had been the first of the neighborhood kids to get drafted. Mr. Nkondo was at the top of the driveway, hosing dead cicadas and watching the arrival of the party guests.

"There's a bunch of other kids," I said.

"I can see that."

"Who are they? From Waldorf?"

"Waldorf, I bet."

Which was a private school known for social progressivism and a cedar-log play structure the size of Disneyland. We had Muslim kids in our school. But if they could afford it, Muslim kids went to Waldorf.

"Forget it," I said.

My best friend had a look on his face like maybe he agreed. We just stood there for a few seconds while our sunscreen scattered and absorbed ultraviolet radiation. Hottest day of summer so far. Meanwhile, Mr. Nkondo had come down his driveway, garden hose still in hand. He had closed down the nozzle, and the water was surging in there, like blood behind a clot.

"Hello, Zeb. Dorian."

"Hi, Mr. N."

He removed his kente-cloth hat, ran his wet hand through his wooly hair, and looked at the scene playing out next door. The lady in the head scarf talking to the driver of the car that had passed us; the kids running up the lawn together. Definitely, all of them Arabic.

"Lemme guess. You two guys are going to a funeral on a beach."

"Pool party," Plaxico said.

Mr. N put the hat back on. "You know those kids?"

"Well," Plaxico said, "we know Abdelkarim."

"Not really," I said.

"We met him the other day."

"Me, too," Mr. N said. "I met him the other day. Can't say it was love at first sight. The kid's kind of, I don't know."

"Yeah," I said.

"So, you got that feeling, too," he said. "Well, let's not rush to judgment. He's been through a lot lately. I told Ry about him the other day. Ryder's been to Najaf. He's been all over the place, and he says there's kids like him everywhere over there. The orphans get recruited, and pretty soon they're blowing themselves into a million pieces. So, maybe it's all good. Help a kid, save some innocent lives. Maybe that's how we get out of this mess. A few lives at a time." He raised the leaking hose to his lips. "And Ryder told me to say hi to you guys."

"Tell him hi back," Plaxico said.

"I will, Zeb."

I knew that Mr. N had been an orphan. From Nigeria. Adopted at the age of one by an American couple. Growing up, his name had been Hendrix Woodworth. Later on, he reclaimed his original Nigerian surname. Went to college, got married, had a son, a really cool teenager who would help us build ramps when we wanted to play X Games, and who still asked about us from all the way over there.

I wondered now.

What if someone had never helped Mr. N?

He had turned the garden hose back on and resumed the work of washing away the nymphal skins and the winged bodies killed by radial tires. As the water hit the blacktop, it atomized, alchemized into a rainbow-flecked spray. I caught up with Plaxico. "I still say forget it," I said.

Mr. B had his arms spread wide, as if to make it easier for us to read the cook apron: GRILL MASTER — THE MAN, THE MYTH, THE LEGEND. He was at the far end of the patio, with Abdelkarim and the three other kids ringed around him. Like a story from the war. Surrounded by brown children; handing out candy. The three kids knew each other. Hanging close, elbows rubbing. Abdelkarim stood off a little. If he was feeling anything, you couldn't tell from the expression on his face.

I remember thinking: there are two of us and four of them.

Plaxico and I were halfway across the patio when another guest arrived, a black girl I'd never seen before. I expected her to gravitate to us. Instead, she went straight for the Arab kids and started doing handshakes.

"You must be Khaleela," said Mr. B.

"Yes, sir."

"*Sir?*" Mr. B gave me and Plaxico a look. "*Sir*, she says. Khaleela, the boys in this hood call me Mr. B. You call me Mr. B. Okay now. Listen carefully because this will be on the exam. Kids from the mosque, meet the kids from the hood. That's Zeb. Next to Zeb, we have Dorian. Boys from the hood, meet the kids from the mosque. Omar, Tarriq, Husain, and Khaleela."

The mosque.

I couldn't believe it. Three out of these four kids had gone to the bathroom in the same stall I had defaced.

"I know you from somewhere," Omar said.

"Me?"

"You go to Sacred Heart?"

"No," I said.

"You all go to Waldorf?" Plaxico asked.

Omar nodded. Khaleela said no, she went to Dorothy Nolan. Plaxico told them where we went.

"You just look familiar," Omar said. "Do I?"

"Not really," I said.

Mr. B seemed happy we were talking. He bent close to Abdelkarim to render the dialogue comprehensible.

"I know," Omar said. "You were in *The Wizard of Oz*."

"Huh?"

"The play. In the park last year. You were the Mayor."

"Of the Munchkins," added Tarriq.

"No," I said.

Omar looked at me. Had he seen me in the mosque? Not the first time, but the second. After I'd confessed, I'd had to return to that place and look the imam in the eye and apologize; and then go back into that bathroom with a scouring pad and heavy duty cleanser and scrub the words away; and then give the entire partition a fresh coat of paint.

"Wait a second," Omar said. He turned to the other kid, Husain, and went off in Arabic. Husain looked at me as if I'd come suddenly into focus. "Na'am, na'am," Husain said. Omar took a step closer to me.

"You do soccer last summer at East Side Rec?"

"Yeah."

"That's it. I knew I knew you from somewhere. Soccer. You were always doing those slide tackles."

Which was bullshit because I'd never done a slide tackle. I'd never been yellow carded in my life. When I told Omar he had me mixed up with somebody else, he said he didn't think so.

We all headed for the pool.

"I think they're thinking of Johnny Iz," Plaxico said.

"I know," I said.

"He's a real dick, that kid."

"And I don't look anything like him."

"Well, you *are* both white."

"Shut up."

"I'm just saying," he said, "all white people pretty much look alike."

Until a few days before, the pool—a basic above-ground model: oval in shape, twenty-something feet long—had been drained and covered. It had been sitting there, taking up space in the backyard, for years. Ever since Mrs. Banfelder had died at the age of sixty from cancer of the skin. Now, not only was chlorinated water sparkling in it again, but a transparent sun dome was covering the entire thing like a missile shield. If you'd been watching from a distance, as Mr. B was, you might have assumed the children under the bubble were having fun. For a while, we all did cannonballs, trying to hit the dome and scare cicadas off the outer surface. We had a semblance of a conversation. How many bugs up there. Two hundred. Five hundred. Khaleela floated on an inner tube, sunglassed, head back, counting. Omar approached from below and capsized her. She surfaced, choking and spitting; and as she shook water from her cornrowed hair, blinking her huge bright eyes, she yelled, "I need mouth-to-mouth!" When Khaleela caught me looking at her, she rolled her eyes and puffed out her cheeks like a blowfish. I went under, eyes closed. Dampened by the water, the sound of the insects flexing their tymbals reminded me of something. What was it? Then it came to me. That tone played on the radio. That cold, musical note reminding us that the next emergency could come at any moment.

We went in for lunch. Grilled veggie burgers, chicken nuggets, and jalapeno poppers, snack chips, and every kind of soda under the sun. We'd been stuffing our faces for a good fifteen minutes when from the computer in the other room came digitally compressed audio of a muezzin chanting the Azan.

"Time for Salat," said Mr. B.

I remembered this from the Islam chapter in Social Studies. Five times a day. The kids from the mosque started whining, but Mr. B said he ran a devout ship and, when it was time to pray, everyone was going to pray.

"Even them?" Omar said. Meaning: me and Plaxico.

"Well, not them."

"We could show them," Khaleela said.

"Show them?" Mr. B said.

"Salat. How we do it."

Mr. B got this look on his face like he was really touched and very happy, like the party just kept getting better and better. He asked Omar and Tarriq and Husain what they thought of this idea, of Zeb and Dorian observing the afternoon prayer. They shrugged okay. Then he asked me and Plaxico what *we* thought. And Plaxico shrugged okay. And then Mr. B turned to Abdelkarim and explained the whole thing in Arabic and presumably asked him what *he* thought of the idea.

And Abdelkarim just sat there.

Same as me.

Same as the other night on the phone. He hadn't wanted to talk to me then. Didn't want me to watch him pray now. I thought of what we'd learned about Mecca in Social Studies. How non-Muslims are not allowed there. How the highway going into that city divides: a road forward for believers; and an exit for people like me. Now, while the muezzin's melancholy chant carried through the house, Mr. B stood over his new son, waiting for him to say okay in one way or another.

"Karim," he urged.

All this time, the kid had been staring down at his plate. Finally, he opened his mouth to speak. A single word.

"No."

It was possibly the first thing he'd said all afternoon. Certainly the first thing I had heard him say. Not "no" in Arabic. "No" in English. Spoken by him, that everyday word sounded new and complicated.

"Excuse us," said Mr. B.

He motioned to Abdelkarim. For a long moment, the boy didn't move. Then did. He followed his new father out of the room. The rest of us stayed at the kitchen table, neither crunching chips nor slurping soda, just sitting quietly while Abdelkarim got lectured at the end of the hall. Khaleela bit her lower lip, sorry for starting the whole thing. The Arab kids listened in like intelligence agents conducting electronic surveillance. They kept squinting their eyes, trying to make out the whispered words. But I think we all knew what Mr. B was telling him.

You aren't over there anymore. You are here. This is America. This is how you act in America.

Down in the basement, a big Persian carpet now on the tile floor and, on the wall, a framed photo of the Grand Mosque.

Omar, Tarriq, Husain, Khaleela, and Abdelkarim stood barefoot on the carpet, facing the photograph. They raised their hands up. Folded their hands on their chests. Bowed. Sat. Knelt and lowered foreheads to the carpet. Speaking Arabic in unison and moving in concert, perfect copies of each other, except when Abdelkarim broke with ancient ritual to wipe tears from his eyes with the back of his hand . . . I knew why we were doing it—the three of us, the nonbelievers, standing there, watching. Same reason my class had gone to the mosque: to understand better, to share.

But we went to the mosque and what happened? I wrote those words in the bathroom. And here we were now, and it seemed to me that just *being* in that basement—not doing anything hateful, not thinking anything hateful—was just as bad.

Plaxico and I should've left after that. We tried to, but Mr. B wouldn't let us. "Home," he said. "Why home? No one wants you to go home." It was perfectly obvious, however, that he was the only one who wanted us to stay. Even Khaleela wanted us to leave. If not for us, she never would've proposed the idea that had thoroughly ruined the day for the kid we were all there to welcome and befriend. In the kitchen, the food had gone cold. A housefly was puddle jumping from one thing to another. We took ice pops outside, and they immediately started to melt like polar caps. Artificial color dripped onto our fingers as we licked. While Plaxico and I stood against the house in a scalene triangle of shade, and Omar, Husain, Tarriq, and Khaleela jockeyed for position under the crank-and-tilt umbrella, Abdelkarim wandered nomadically in the solarized interspace of the patio.

"Hey," Omar said. "Aryan." He was talking to me.

"*Dor*ian," I said.

"How come you're not in soccer camp this summer?"

I just looked at him.

"Because they suspended you is what I heard."

"I'm not that kid," I said

Omar laughed, as if he couldn't believe I was still playing that. It was the time of day, one o'clock or so, when you started to feel a little crazy: the heat making you dizzy and the noise of the cicadas like schizophrenic voices in your head.

"And don't call me that," I said.

"Call you what?"

"You know what. Am I calling *you* names?"

"You were last summer."

"Are you deaf," I said. "I'm not that kid."

When Plaxico told him he was thinking of Johnny Iz, Omar told Plaxico to not tell him who he was thinking of, Khaleela told us all to just cut it out, and Omar told her to shut up, which is when I told Omar if he said one more rude thing to her, I would knock the towel off his fucking head.

"What?"

"You heard me."

"*What*, you fucking Aryan?"

"You heard me, Towel Head."

What came next would puzzle me for years, the way I just stood there and sucked my popsicle and let Omar walk right up to me and punch me in the stomach.

For a few long seconds, I couldn't get any air. I remember thinking, while my diaphragm spasmed, of Khaleela's joke from the pool. I need mouth-to-mouth. Now I saw her across the patio. Not moving, a hand sort of shielding her face. None of us moving. In my memory, those moments have always been behind glass: we're all life-size models of ourselves arranged before a painted backdrop of a domed swimming pool and green trees, children from another time, from days of hate and plague.

Then the scene is in motion. I'm breathing again and everyone's yelling in Arabic and English. I'm curling my hands into fists. Catching Omar hard on the jaw before Tarriq and Husain get me by the arms and neck. It came out of nowhere. First a flash of blindness, then the pain across my face, as if a hard grounder had taken a bad hop. Then the spate of blood. When my vision came back, there he was—Abdelkarim—with this look in his eyes. Hopeless and starved. Like no matter how many times he hit me, it would never be enough to make up for what he'd lost.

Still, he drew his arm back to hit me again.

I didn't want to go home. I knew what my family would think: I had started it. At first, I wasn't sure if I had or not. "What the hell happened," Mr. B was saying. He was talking to me, but the answers were coming from everyone else. Omar kept saying that I had used a racial slur. Plaxico said Omar had used one first. Husain said the slurs and the slide tackling had started a whole year ago. Plaxico explained they were thinking of Johnny Iz.

As for Abdelkarim, he was nowhere in sight.

I got to my feet and started walking. Plaxico caught up with me on the front lawn. "D," he said. "Where you going?"

"Not home," I informed him.

"Then where?"

At the foot of the hill, there was a culvert, a big concrete pipe underlying the road. When we were little, we'd pretend we were caving or trapped in a time tunnel. I had outgrown those games, but it was still a good place to disappear into. Now, crawling in a ways, I dipped my hands into the trickle of water and carefully dabbed at my face. Fat lip, one eye swollen nearly shut. The kid had gone completely ape shit on me—and I had done *nothing*, said *nothing* to him. I looked at my fingers. Red, like I'd been painting with them. But I hadn't started it. Omar had called me Aryan. Which is what some kids at school had started calling me after the thing at the mosque. A white person. A racist. Worse than that. I am not one of them, I thought. Sobbing now. Not one of them. Those kids have got me mixed up with somebody else.

I remembered that my parents had plans. A music festival with a lineup of ancient indie rock bands who'd been big around the turn of the century. I went home and poured out a teaspoon of cherry-flavored pain reliever and checked my phone. Two voice mails from Mr. B. There was something frightening about his name, there, on my phone. Like the other night, but more abnormal. I played the first message, left at 3:41. Someone crying. Abdelkarim. Not just crying. Wailing. Screaming. And Mr. B shouting at him in Arabic—in a voice I'd never heard him use, which made me think of the photographs in his basement, of a soldier young and strong and armed. Then he spoke, an old man again, to me: "Dorian, Abdelkarim has something to say to you." But the kid wouldn't take the phone. The rest was Arabic. Something like: You will take this phone. No. You will apologize to this boy. No, I *won't*. And then Mr. B was shouting again and Abdelkarim was freaking again.

End of message.

I'd heard plenty of temper tantrums in my life. One time, I'd seen a kid with intermittent explosive disorder go nuclear in the school gymnasium. This was different. To me, this didn't sound like any kind of anger. It sounded like grief. I just sat there, staring at my phone. Too scared to listen to the second message.

❧

Around eleven o'clock the next morning, I faced my parents. In accord with a plan made the night before, my brother had been debriefing them in the kitchen, outlining the situation and giving his own sober analysis of what had happened and who was really responsible. Now he called, "In the left caw-nah, weighing in at just und-ah ninety-six pounds, Daw-rian Wakefield!" Still in boxer shorts and a T-shirt, I walked out of my room and down the hall, feeling like a total ass.

I stepped into the doorway of the kitchen and slouched against the jamb.

Smell of burning toast.

Sound of toaster discharging burnt toast.

My mother took one look at me, and covered her eyes with one hand. As for my father, I knew instantly he was sorry. When he got sorry, he took off his eyeglasses and held them with the silver arms folded into an X and stared into the astigmatic distance. He looked terrible. Like someone who'd forgotten for a night that he wasn't young anymore. Now it was morning and his eyes were full of blood and there were children.

He said sit. Talk. I told the whole story. Voice steady, tone neutral. When I was through, my father put his glasses back on. My mother stood up and went to the window as if she didn't want to see me, even in her peripheral vision.

"So, you used a racial slur," she said.

"Yes, but—"

"To his face you called him that." Now she turned around; she was crying, and the sight of it shocked me into silence.

"Mom," my brother said.

"You shut up," she said. "I don't want to hear any cruel humor from you. And you," she said to me. "I'm sick about you, Dorian. This makes me sick."

"Look," my father said, "they ganged up on him."

"Three against one," my brother said.

"Four," I specified.

My father took a deep breath. "We should probably report this."

"Report," my mother said.

"To the police."

"No way."

"They beat him up," my father said. "There could be a criminal charge."

"We are not calling the police," my mother said. "We are not going to get Abdelkarim mixed up with the police."

"What would happen?" I said.

"They'd probably just stack him in a naked human pyramid."

"God damn it, Cliff."

"Sorry."

My father reached out and squeezed my arm. "Want some breakfast?"

"Okay."

"This conversation isn't over," my mother said, more to my father than to me. But he didn't pay her any mind. He opened a carton of organic brown eggs and commenced breaking them into a bowl.

Since the thing at the mosque, my mother had scarcely touched me. She had never been, in my memory, an affectionate person. During those years when a child wakes in the morning and charts a direct course for the bed of his parents, my father was always the one who opened his arms and made a place for me to shelter in. I knew the smell and density of his body. But my mother had always stayed just out of my reach. For the last three months, my mother had been more than distant; she'd been cold. It scared me. Any day, something catastrophic could happen without warning; and for the rest of my life, it would make perfect sense, how we'd drifted apart, more and more, until finally there was no way to come close again.

I got the mower out of the garage. The only way to clear my mind back then—the only way to slow the world down—was to cut the lawn. I put the battery in and turned the key and shifted into forward and started pushing. The drone of the engine spun a kind of cocoon around me.

Across the expanse of the lawn, strewn over the flats and the knolls: cicadas without number. Nothing to do but go over them.

The blade spun indifferently, slicing the grass at three inches and sucking into its updraft the bodies of the living and the dead; and a terrible thrill went through me at the sight of a thickly populated area, as with a video game my parents had forbidden me to ever play again, in which you piloted a stealth attack plane over virtual miles of deserts and mountains, over villages and cities, firing air-to-ground missiles at royal palaces and mosques, at houses, and at people turbaned or scarfed . . . The mower droned and my hands absorbed the vibrations of the motor. As I paced the property that afternoon, I might have been imagining any kind of revenge. But the scene in my mind was this: Me speaking to him in Arabic. Asking him to explain. Why. If a person never did anything to you. If you don't know anything about him.

And then the atmosphere changed its mind, and very quickly the sky went dark and a wind began to thrash the leaves on the trees. Flash of lightning. Then, several seconds later, a sonic boom so loud it made the bruises on my face hurt. By the time I got the mower into the garage, I was soaked. I don't know how long I was there, looking out at the rain, listening to the trance loop of the storm, before my father appeared beside me.

"Listen," he said.

"What . . ."

"The cicadas."

"I know," I said. "They don't chorus in the rain." I wandered around the garage and found a tennis ball and started bouncing it on the concrete floor.

"How are you feeling?" he finally asked.

"Fine."

"Angry, I bet. Which you have every right to be. At them and us. If we hadn't made you go, this wouldn't have happened."

I looked at him. It was clear, from his tone and the expression on his face, that this was his view of things—not my mother's.

"This is your call," he said.

"What is?"

"What to do now. You remember what I said before. You want to go to the police, I'll take you there."

I was shaking, just the slightest bit, from the chill of wet clothes and the fear of what might happen next.

"What about Mom?"

"Don't worry about your mother. Your mother's problems and your mother's agenda are not your concern."

"Okay."

He nodded, as if we'd reached some sort of agreement. The rain beat violently on the driveway.

"By the way," he said. "You never told me. Did you find the photo?"

"What photo?"

"That picture you wanted. Of us on the beach."

I shook my head no. He asked if I'd opened every file on the drive, and I said I had, and it hadn't been there. "That's strange," he said, looking into the storm. "I wonder where it could be."

❧

That evening, after the storm, when Mr. Banfelder answered his door and found me standing on the porch, he got the strangest look on his face. He had told us stories about the boys over there. How you could never be sure when a kid came up to you, wanting something, if he might be wearing a vest under his clothes packed with explosives and nails. The look on his face made me think of that.

"Mr. D," he said.

"Is it Salat? If it's prayer time, I can come back."

He opened the screen door. Exoskeletons dangling from the wire mesh like tiny paper lanterns. I sat on the step when he told me to; and as he lowered himself down beside me, I found myself looking at his bare feet, at toenails sprouting a yellow fungus.

"Damn it," he said. "I'm sorry."

"Me, too."

"But you came here to say something. You took some time to think this through and now you've got something to say and you come over in person to say it. You're solid, Dorian. Permission to speak freely, soldier."

I took a deep breath. "Can I talk to him?"

He got that look on his face again, like maybe he didn't trust me. Then he nodded, like I was the most solid person he'd ever met, and rose to his fungal feet and went inside. Across the street, my house was a shadow in the dusk. I'd left a light on in my room. I could make out the shape of a baseball pennant on the wall, and imagined having an hallucination in which I saw myself there, coming close to the window and looking across the street. Behind me now, the screen door opened. I was surprised and embarrassed to see that, at the hour of eight with night having scarcely fallen, Abdelkarim was already in pajamas. We sat. I at Mr. Banfelder's left and Abdelkarim at his right.

"Marhaban," said Abdelkarim.

"Mar-ban," I said.

"If it's cool with you," Mr. B said to me, "Karim would like to begin. By making an apology."

"That's cool."

Mr. B said something in Arabic; then Abdelkarim said, "Assif," which I figured meant "sorry." Then after a delay, he spoke a much longer sentence, and Mr. B said that what Abdelkarim had said was that he was sorry for hitting me three times in the face when I wasn't able to defend myself or fight back. I suppose it was the language of his body that created an impression of sincerity: he wasn't looking at me or looking away, but gazing over the lawn, where he appeared to be seeing more in the gathering dark than the twinkling signals of fireflies. After a few seconds, he added some words that his father didn't seem to be expecting.

"Hasan," said Mr. B, laying a hand on his son's shoulder. "Good." Then he turned to me. "He wants to compensate you."

"What?"

"He wants to give you half of his allowance for the rest of the summer."

"That's really nice," I said. "But—"

"Now just be open-minded for a second. This is ancient Islamic stuff. Over there, when this kind of thing happens, you're looking at either a century-long blood feud, or the parties sit down and talk and drink tea." He broke off to address Abdelkarim, who got up right away and went into the house. "He's getting some tea. The wrongdoer makes an apology to the victim and offers money. In this case, we're talking roughly . . . forty bucks."

"Mr. B."

"You want a blood feud?"

"No."

"Then take the money. That is," he said, "assuming, well, you know, assuming you accept the apology."

"I accept the apology," I said.

Mr. Banfelder was looking right at me. Though the light was fading, I could see a dew of emotion in his eyes, which made him look very old. Too old, I thought, to be starting a family. To the door came Abdelkarim, balancing on a tray three glasses of iced tea. Mr. B opened the door and took the tray, announcing to his son that the conflict had been resolved. In Arabic, Abdelkarim said, Good, I am happy about that. Same thing he'd said the other night about my coming to the party. Only tonight he seemed to mean it.

We sat and drank the sweet and minty tea while the sky darkened and the bioluminescent flashes of the fireflies became too many to count.

"You know what," Mr. B said.

"What," I said.

"You two give me hope."

He repeated the sentiment in Arabic. Then he put one arm around him and one arm around me; and while the fireflies drifted like a magic dust, I tried to find a voice for what I had come over to say in the first place. That I felt I could understand. Because I had lost someone, too. But as I sat there staring at my house, grayscale in the gloaming and curving toward darkness, I couldn't do anything but drink the tea.

FALSE POSITIVE

When the girl appears at the door, Kevin is doing the homework for birthing class—rehearsing with Nora the first stage of labor—and trying to not think about the test: a long needle through Nora's belly into the fluid surrounding the fetus. Try to not think about it. The first test might have been a false positive. He keeps using this term. False positive. As if to prove his mastery of the concept. Then the doorbell. Nora remains on all fours, her belly almost touching the rug. Kevin goes to answer. On the front porch stands a girl, maybe nine, maybe ten.

Hi, Kevin says.

Hi.

He figures she is selling something for her school or seeking sponsors for a charity walk. He can remember, as a kid, going door-to-door. The associated emotions, the fear of asking something of strangers, has always stuck in his memory. He feels a prick of sympathy. He wants to give her money. That's when he notices the backpack at her feet (pink and glossy, prettied up with the image of a cartoon kitty cat) and the way her black hair is hanging flat and oily around her shoulders. The faded look of someone who has just completed a hard bus trip.

Is your name, she says, Kevin Johnson?

Johnston.

Nora, from the top of the stairs: Kev, who is it?

The girl looks past him, up the staircase, along the wall hung with photographs, matted and framed and rising in altitude like the steps. When she asks him who's that, and he tells her it's his wife, the girl gives him a look: part puzzlement, part disapproval. He has seen these eyes before—and also the face they're a part of. He knows this face, this girl.

And the girl knows him. As an albatross or a salmon knows home. She knows he is the one. The man who knew her mother. Though he was not with her mother for long. And the girl understood nothing back then. In those days, she floated in a darkness, in a fluid, though she was also able (some invisible part of her was) to wander a certain distance, like a balloon on a cord, in what she now knows to be the air. She was not a person then. Not human. But a strange, ugly creature. Glowing dimly. A pulsing jellyfish. She can't believe she was ever one of those things. No wonder so many people don't want them. Now she moves a foot forward.

Can I come in?

She wants to know if she can come in. Kevin's not sure what to do. If he were home alone (middle-aged man, wayward prepubescent girl), he'd never consider it. Or maybe he would. Because the kid is clearly in some kind of trouble. How wrong it would be, on a basic human level, to *not* take her in. You take her in; you call the police. Luckily, his wife is here. He moves aside so the visitor can enter the foyer.

Kev?

Someone's here, he says.

Nora appears at the top of the stairs, places one hand on the banister, the other on her belly.

Hello, someone.

The girl doesn't respond, just stares up at the pregnant lady on the second floor. Nora tries a smile. It's genuine, drawn from a well of tenderness intended for a different child, but the well is deep enough, full enough.

No dice.

Turning to Kevin, the girl asks, Should I take my shoes off first?

Initially, it's a feeling of déjà vu: a girl at the door, pink backpack, this girl with these eyes. Standing in the foyer with her feels like watching a defective video disc, as if time is just a lot of digital data subject to random skipping. But the sensation doesn't peak and fade. Only gets sharper and harder to understand.

In the living room, he watches the girl pad across the hardwood floor. She wanders toward the baby swing. The swing has been there for three weeks already, loaded with batteries, waiting. The girl gives it a gentle push, and the ghost of a smile appears for a moment on those tiny chapped lips.

Kevin?

He turns to his wife. A look of goodwill is still on her face, but so are the obvious questions. Who is she? What is she doing here? He finally says in a murmur: I think she's lost. Nora nods, seeming to notice only now the oily hair, the dry lips, the grayish hollows under the eyes. Kevin stays put while his wife eases herself into an armchair a few feet from the girl and asks her name.

Mizuko, she says.

Mizuko. Good, okay. You look thirsty. How about some water?

Is it pure?

Well, it's filtered.

Okay.

I'll get it, Kevin says.

I'll go with you, the girl says; and before he can object, she's scooting across the room, taking the long way around the coffee table to avoid going anywhere near his wife.

She does not hate him. She's not angry. Some are. Not her. She doesn't want to be like that. Not here to do any harm. At the river, she has always piled her stones and sung to him without any bitterness. But this lady—this lady with the jellyfish inside—makes her feel stupid and broken. She follows her father into the kitchen. Father. She has said the word many times, more than she can possibly count. She has piled so many thousands of stones for him. Still, to call him this, even in her mind, seems unnatural, a kind of mistake. He keeps looking at her. But only curiously, confusedly. It wasn't like this when she found her mother. The lady is the difference.

Her belly is big.

They want to keep it.

In the kitchen, Kevin removes the pitcher from the fridge, selects a glass, fills it part way. The girl watches these actions from a distance, from behind the breakfast table, where dried flowers (the same shade of pink as the girl's backpack) rise out of a slender vase. When he places the water on the table, she takes it at once in two hands and drinks, staring at him over the rim of the glass. It's more than the eyes. It's skin tone, bone structure. The resemblance is uncanny. As soon as he saw her, ten years slipped out from under him.

So, he finally says, where do you live?

Nowhere really. She speaks into the glass; so her voice sounds disguised, like a voice warped by computer, as if her identity needs to be protected.

Nowhere, huh?

Through the doorway, Kevin can see Nora. She's moving to the other end of the apartment, into the bedroom, where the telephone is located. She closes the door soundlessly. The girl says, The river. And it takes him a second to understand that she's giving a better answer to his question.

Which river is that?

I don't know the name. But there's no water in it, only stones.

He has no idea what place she is referring to. Can't recall having seen any dry riverbeds in the surrounding suburbs. There's been a lot of rain this summer, some flooding.

What's your baby? she asks.

Excuse me?

That lady is pregnant.

I know.

So what is it? A boy or a girl?

We don't know yet, he replies.

Again, she brings the glass to her lips and stares at him. The information seems to displease her, as the sight of his wife did when she first entered the apartment. Suddenly, he doesn't want this girl in the house. She's starting to scare him. The next day, they have the amnio, and only now is it really coming clear—how the future might be bright or dark depending on the outcome. The girl's appearance, her presence, feels like something he might interpret in retrospect as a sign, a bad omen. He's not superstitious. Still, Kevin is glad his wife is calling the police, and he wants them to hurry up and get here.

When the girl looks back into the living room, there it is, the fetus, floating and pulsing in the air. She doesn't exactly see it. It's not visible, it's just *there*. The lady is still in the back room. Her baby is wandering. The girl can sense when it reaches the end of its invisible cord; it jerks like a balloon on a string. Funny stupid thing. More than a jellyfish. It's further along than that. Half human. There are toes. Sprouting seed of a heart. Now she walks over to where the thing is floating. She can tell right away that it's a boy, and she can tell also that there's something wrong with him. She knows ones like this at the river. They aren't so common, but there are plenty of them. Their heads are too big, they're missing their spines. They grow, but they don't get any different. They can't learn to pile the rocks. Can't say mother, can't say father.

She is standing in the living room, staring up into empty space. Not blankly—with concentration, as if there's something worthy of study hanging from the ceiling. Kevin wonders if the girl is delusional, posttraumatic. He's been hoping that she's not really lost, just separated from her parents. Maybe she was on one of those tours, those amphibious vehicles that start in the river then lumber through the city's drab history. He asks her. She doesn't seem to understand the question. No, the story is darker than that.

Look at her.

She looks like a child who's been missing for years. As for the resemblance. Certainly she is Japanese. Part Japanese. He has seen girls like this before, and they always create the same linkage in his mind. They make his heart stop for a second—sometimes they make him shake—and afterwards, he feels guilty and igno- rant, because he knows it's nothing, this mental association, but a kind of racial profiling. Still, this girl. Looks so much like theirs might have looked. If they'd had her. If they'd had her and she'd gotten lost, been abducted, gone missing for years, and suddenly resurfaced after who knows what. She would look exactly like this.

The lady comes out of the back room, holding her belly. As if the whole baby, the real baby, is in there. The girl almost blurts something out. He's not normal, you know. Is that what she's really here for, to bring bad news? Don't be like that. If you tell them, they'll think you caused it. And she did not cause it. She didn't even know until she got here: her father is having another baby with a woman not her mother.

When his wife emerges from the bedroom, Kevin thinks again of tomorrow's appointment. The results of the first test came back only yesterday; and much of yesterday they spent on the Internet, scrolling through parenting websites, searching for reassuring information. They found a wealth of it. A lot of people out there have received the same news, only to learn that it was inaccurate. A false positive. Still, he was up most of the night. Thinking of what they might do if the second test confirms the first.

What'cha looking at?

No sooner has Nora joined the girl in staring at the ceiling than the girl moves away again, a forest creature maintaining a safe distance. Back to the baby swing. Kevin wishes she'd stay away from the thing. He already wishes they hadn't bought it. He feels foolish for having taken it out of the box and assembled it. Now here it is for this girl to touch, to leave her fingerprints on. He suddenly remembers a dream from last night, in which he'd taken the swing out to the curb and left it with the rest of the trash. His heart is beating very quickly now.

Mizuko, Nora says. What kind of name is that?

What do you think?

Hmm. Japanese?

The girl shrugs, as if this is only one of several correct answers. Then says, matter-of-factly: My mother's Japanese.

There's a long silence, a weird silence. He and this girl. For a moment, he is convinced that they are thinking of the same woman, seeing the same woman in memory. Kevin can hardly remember the face. It all happened so long ago! He can't see any of it, really. The experience has slipped past the edge of the visible spectrum.

I'm Asian American, the girl says, making the empty seat of the swing rock back and forth. My father's American.

There. Finally. Wasn't sure if she'd be able to say it. Now that she has, part of her wishes she'd kept her mouth shut. What does she want anyway? Doesn't her mother light incense for her at the temple? Every month now her mother goes there and kneels at the memorial and cries very softly at the thought of her. What more? She should leave her father alone. Go back. The idea makes her eyes burn. She turns around and looks at him. Standing in the doorway to the kitchen. A man wearing old blue jeans. Hair hanging down around his shoulders. He could use a shave. Maybe this is all she wanted.

To see him.

Now leave him alone. Leave. She's trying to remember where she left her pack. Suddenly, she's in a rush, wishing she had never come. Then, three sharp knocks on the glass panes of the front door.

The officer at the door is the one who patrols on a bike. Kevin doesn't know his name, has never spoken to him, but often sees him engaged in friendly conversation with homeowners or mediating a dispute between the people who wander up and down these streets looking strung out and hungry, not unlike the girl in question.

Mr. Johnson?

Johnston.

I'm Officer Pratt.

Kevin leads him upstairs. The living room is empty; and

again there is the sense of time slipping, of everything coming unordered.

She was just here, Kevin says. Nora!

Out here!

A small porch off the second bedroom is where they've gone. Nora has her flowers out here. There's a patio table and a charcoal grill. No stairs to the ground, however; and that's what it seems the girl was looking for. She has lost her surreal composure. She seems very childlike now. When the officer steps onto the porch, her lips start to tremble. Somehow, Kevin knows immediately that it's not a matter of fear. The emotion has nothing really to do with the cop, a soft-featured stranger in a cycling uniform. Nora made the call. But the person the girl looks at, very deliberately, is Kevin. As if he's the traitor. And his own emotion? The heat behind his eyes? Has got nothing to do with her. Nothing to do with anything real. The future is always dividing like a cell. Every day, something new is conceived without ever actually beginning. Those other lives, the ones you don't choose, are only slightly less imaginary than a dream.

They go inside while the officer talks to the girl on the porch. They sit in their living room as if it's some kind of a waiting room.

Poor thing, Nora says.

Yeah.

She just bolted like a scared kitten.

Across the room, the girl's pack is lying on the floor. Kevin had forgotten about this object, which now seems vivid with meaning. Impulsively, he goes over and unzips it. What was he expecting? Something dramatic, something fantastic. There's nothing inside but a few dozen little smooth stones.

Name, address, names of parents, telephone number. Mostly, she says nothing. Looking away from the policeman. Don't you understand? I'm nothing. I'm no one. Never was.

That night, Kevin can't sleep. He's worried about the amnio, worried about the girl. Too restless to stay in bed. There's leftover take-out food in the fridge. While he eats it, he looks up the number for the police department. Almost picks up the phone. Probably, by now they have located her in some database. She might already be on her way back to wherever she started from, wherever she got stolen from. A lost girl like that. Who knows what she's been through? He's not sure he wants to know.

Back in bed, he places a hand on his wife's belly.

What time is it? she asks.

After two.

You smell like plum sauce.

I had a craving, he says.

She rolls onto her back. You know what I read the other day? Some women get cravings for nonfood items. Dirt, for instance.

Dirt.

Laundry soap, cigarette butts. Weird, huh?

Very.

Though the room is dark, a diffuse light filters through the drawn curtains. It comes from the floodlight on a neighbor's back porch. He can make out his wife's features. Can see that she has been awake, too.

Didn't like me much, Nora says.

Huh?

That girl. It was weird, the way she kept gravitating to you. But you know the weirdest thing.

What?

She sort of looked like you.

He lies there, still. It all happened so long ago, but it's coming back to him now. The airport, the gate. Your loved ones, anyone, could come up to the gate in those days, and the closer you came together to the point of departure, the harder the separation would be. When he finally let go of her, it felt like a ripping, a tearing, as of a muscle—only it wasn't flesh tearing but something more like a spirit. He did think of the abortion then, which had been performed a week earlier; and as he moved down the jet bridge, trying to not look back, he couldn't help comparing himself with the fetus, a thing torn violently away, drawn into a tunnel and then carried away to another world.

Hey, Nora says. What gives?

Nothing.

Hey, Kev. Hey.

She strokes his face. He can see her eyes, and they are wide open. He feels certain that she could understand almost anything.

It's just this test, he says.

I know.

What if he slips with the needle?

That never happens.

Never?

But they've been over this. The small risk of miscarriage, the very negligible risk that the needle may harm the baby. Kevin feels selfish for revisiting these concerns. They will have the test. This much has already been decided. They have to know, one way or the other. Probably, the first test was a false positive. There's a good chance of that, a good chance. And if not, if the second test confirms the first—what will they do? More than needles, more than missing chromosomes, Kevin fears this question. In the darkness before dawn, everything gets mixed up together. The tests, the girl, the past. As he fades in and out of sleep, his thoughts become bizarre. He keeps imagining that the girl was his daughter, the one that isn't finished growing inside his wife, and he feels a terror at having let her be taken away.

GREEN WORLD

My new defense attorney is a young and tireless idealist. She files appeals the way some people knock back drinks or smoke cigarettes. I believe she regards me as more than a client. I believe she sees me as a symbol and a metaphor, and my case as a kind of historical fulcrum. Also, I believe she has a crush on me. It is clear that she is confused by these feelings. They threaten her professional sense of self. They hint at something dark at her core, a previously unglimpsed motivation for her involvement with the lowest of the doomed. Each day, we meet at the glass wall to discuss her hopeless attempts to disable the mechanism of justice.

"You look pretty today," I tell her. "In that suit."

A bloom of color in the cheeks. An attempt at a chastising stare, her little blue eyes rising like little blue moons over the horizon of her eyeglasses.

"Those frames," I say.

"Armani."

"I thought so. They give you a look of severe and erotic intellectualism."

"They're supposed to make me less attractive."

"A beauty like yours can't be disguised, Liza."

"Stop flirting," she says. "You're a condemned man."

"Boy," I correct her.

Clack! Clack! Pow pow pow! Clack! Clack!

This is the sound of my typewriter. Of metal arms, dampened by soft inky ribbon, striking a plane of white. I am thirteen years old, and I have resided in this cell since the time of my eleventh birthday. On that festive morning, my biological mother appeared with a chocolate-frosted cupcake impaled by a tiny baby-blue candle. Forgive and forget, it silently said. Bury the hatchet. I indulged her with a brief pantomime of eye closing, wish making, and blowing out of an imaginary flame. I opened my gift: a brightly colored kazoo. An instrument, she claims, I'd adored in the days before we parted company. She lit a long mentholated cigarette, plastic curlers nesting like giant centipedes in her hair, the chair beneath her creaking like a ship on the high seas. When it comes to this woman, I can't help but feel some disappointment; when thrown, at a green age, surprisingly and squarely into the public eye, one wishes for a leaner and more thoroughbred lineage. My myriad foster parents, I can tell you, are hardly more aristocratic; certainly those subpoenaed and called to the stand at my trial were desperate-looking people who seemed to have good reason to lie and were often tricked into telling the truth. Apparently, if we can believe testimony given under oath, my early years were troubled ones. I don't remember any of them. Not a thing about the world I'd closed my eyes on; and as I sat at the table of my defense, listening to day after day of examination and cross-examination, the eyes in the courtroom were shining all around me like the stars of some teary galaxy, and I, too, felt the urge to cry for the boy they were talking about, whoever he was.

My trial, conducted in a less-than-orderly fashion over the course of several weeks in the jurisdiction of X, is considered by many to have been a travesty of justice. My state-appointed counsel, a man with a fascinating birthmark completely shadowing his left ear, seemed unfamiliar with the relevant cases and statutes and was consistently unprepared for the day's litigation. From time to time, during the prosecution's lengthier occupations of the floor, he would drift off into a reverie that was not an indicator of complicated legal strategizing but of simple somnolence, as evidenced by the thin string of drool that dangled, noose-like, from the corner of his mouth. Ultimately he put me in mind of the duelist who, favored with the first shot, opts chivalrously to fire into the air. As for the prosecuting attorney, the man clearly has a long and distinguished career to look forward to as both a practicing lawyer and a writer of legal thrillers. His closing argument was a work of oratorical genius, cinematic in scope and Dostoyevskian in length; and I must say that, by the time he concluded, even I found myself coming around to his point of view. Shortly after my incarceration, he visited me here, in my new home. We met at the glass wall. He, as always, was flaw-lessly groomed and dressed; I, alas, had not had a shower, and the orange uniform of my criminal constituency was clashing miserably with my first outbreak of acne. He wanted to be sure that there were no hard feelings. He wanted to make clear that, in another reality, we might very well have been friends, and he would have argued the case for my innocence with all the vigor and seeming conviction with which he'd argued the case for my guilt. I understood, of course. I told him that, in my opinion, we all follow the road laid down before us; and all those roads have been trod before, so many times that the bricks underfoot are cracked and worn smooth; and yet, still, we find our way, be the path direct or circuitous, to a common destination. He nodded with a scholarly gravity. I mentioned my new legal counsel. Attractive, erudite, alert. A partner-to-be in a top-notch metropolitan firm who had agreed to waive all fees for her services. He said he knew her well. A woman whose passion for justice is rivaled only by her passion for deeply penetrating acts of physical love.

As you all undoubtedly know by now, the film adaptation of this sad and stormy saga will soon be on its way to a theater near you, starring, as your humble author . . . well, his household name escapes me at the moment, but I am certain you know him. A boy-man. Sandy haired. Young and dashing. An actor whose professional range enables him to portray both romantic lead and idiot savant. I myself must admit to a girlish crush, one of those attractions that begins and ends with the airbrushed image, straying perhaps into the storybook terrain of a midafternoon cuddle, but never—not once, I promise you—approaching the shower room fantasies of violent sodomy broadcast up and down the corridor during his visit by a startling percentage of my peers. He arrived on a Tuesday and stayed until the following Monday, living among us like a missionary from some mythic civilization, wearing our clothes, eating our food, telling us stories about life in his world. His beach house in Malibu, recently featured in *Architectural Digest*. His steamy love affair with an older Academy Award Nominated Actress. Leaning against the bars of his borrowed cell and aiming his little prison-issued mirror in my direction, he spoke of the unremitting assaults by camera, the plague of the Hollywood paparazzi, the crisis of intrusive journalism.

"They're like urban sewer rats," he said. "Hiding. Carrying disease."

"You don't look much like me," I said.

"Have you ever been to the Naked City, Sasha?"

"Will they dye your hair?"

"What?"

"Your hair," I said. "It's blond. Mine's black."

"They'll dye it. They'll make a little prosthetic scar for right here, paint a little acne on my cheek."

A few scattered comments from the cell block about our visitor's hair, about true blondness and the search for it in a dark locked room where a pretty actor boy could scream and scream and never be heard. For some reason, this particular brand of heckling seeped into me like dampness. It chilled my epidermis and gave me a sensation of snow falling between my legs. When I looked back at our guest, fixing his reflected image in my little mirror, he seemed distant and melancholy; and I imagined holding his head to my chest, stroking his blond hair, and making the poisonous voices go away.

"What are you thinking about?" I asked.

"My girlfriend."

"Oh."

His smooth, tanned forehead came to rest against the cold metal bars; and he drifted into a tale of dinners, shopping trips, and gondola rides ruined by rabid photographers. He spoke of basic human rights and our culture's rampant disrespect for the private lives of public figures, while from the end of the corridor, with the humdrum reliability of a geyser, John Milton Luzinski delivered his midmorning quota of reproductive fluid, making the usual breathy demands of imaginary female hostages.

It was only a few mornings ago that Mr. Stearns appeared at my cell—bright and early, in his spotless, perfectly pressed uniform—and, cuffing my hands, escorted me, in an uncharacteristic silence, down the corridor, past the curious and careworn faces of my peers, past the guard station, and through a maze of blank, seemingly soundproof hallways that terminated at a heavy gray door. Here, time seemed to stand still. My ear was nearly level with my companion's belly, whose digestive murmurings evoked things epic and primeval, subterranean lava exploding through the ancient oceans and cooling into continental land masses. "Mr. Stearns," I said, "you've been eating beef again." A moment later, the door buzzed open. An overwhelming burst of light. I blinked and shielded my eyes—somewhat melodramatically, somewhat biblically—until Mr. Stearns offered to lend me his imported sunglasses. The chaotic radiance lifted like a curtain. There were the prison walls garnished with curlicues of shiny electrified wire. Fiery leaves scattered on the ground and coming loose from surrounding trees. Birdsong. A plump, red-breasted robin extracting a worm from a plot of grass. Flowers turning their heads eastward, still heavy with sleep, to be warmed by the young sun.

To be outdoors in the crisp cool of autumn!

How light and buoyant my heart felt, swelling balloon-like in my chest; and for a moment I lost myself, and it seemed I was walking down a suburban lane, schoolbooks in one arm and a bag lunch in the other, the impression of a mother's kiss still fresh on my cheek and a paternal shadow merging with mine on the ground, slipping effortlessly over the scudding whispering leaves, while up ahead the school bus idled patiently, door ajar, with children moving and humming inside like as many bees in a honeycombed hive. Too soon did we reach the steps of a small brick building. Mr. Stearns removed the sunglasses and, brandishing a pocket comb, raked my hair into a semblance of order while I gazed up at the nearby guard tower, realizing suddenly how strange and unprecedented this all was. Inside, we ascended a broad staircase to the second floor, where a door with a frosted window stood open a crack. Mr. Stearns trilled his knuckles upon the glass. A baritonal response from inside. Then the door swung open to reveal the warden seated at a massive mahogany desk, flanked by two windows throwing identical trapezoids of sunlight onto the blood-red carpet. On the wall behind him hung a photograph, nearly as large as the desk itself, in an elaborate wooden frame. A decimated forest. The fallen bodies of a half-dozen giant trees stacked in pyramidal fashion on the flatbed of an eighteen-wheeled truck. Two men, as insignificant and unreal as little toy figures, standing at the rear end of the vehicle. The sky above a powdery blue.

"Good morning, Sasha."

"Good morning, sir."

As Mr. Stearns guided me to a large armchair, I noticed on the warden's desk, resting beneath his long strong fingers, a mustard-yellow envelope.

"Sleep well?" he asked.

"Like a log, sir."

"Let me come straight to the point, my boy."

"Yes, sir."

"Sasha, my boy, in the two years you've been here, we've all become very fond of you."

"Thank you, sir."

"Not just the men, but the staff as well . . . and I, myself."

"The feeling is mutual, sir. All things considered, I can't imagine having a more supportive atmosphere in which to pay my debt to society."

As I completed this sentence, the heavy hand of Mr. Stearns weighed down on my neck with the reassuring warmth of a freshly baked ham. Glancing up, I caught him in the act of wiping a jewel-like tear from his cheek. As for the warden, his posture and facial expression put me in mind of a patriot gazing at the flag of his country on some historic and sentimental holiday. His fingers were undergoing a series of nervous conjoinings, making psychoanalytical shadows on the desk and the envelope. Peaked roof. Church with steeple. Twenty-two-caliber handgun.

"I see you have an envelope there, sir."

"Yes, my boy."

A good minute elapsed; the ham settled solidly on my shoulder, and the shadow fingers twisted themselves into grotesque abstractions over that envelope, which resembled nothing so much as an announcement of one's privileged status in some nationwide million-dollar sweepstakes. I met the warden's eyes, his sky-blue irises misting over with a sad and terrible intention, and felt suddenly like a dog, some helpless bed-wetting dog, abandoned in a remote and faraway place.

"It's from the governor," I said, "isn't it?"

"I'm profoundly sorry, my boy."

He picked it up and transferred it to my shackled hands, explaining that this personal meeting was highly irregular, but under the circumstances et cetera et cetera. I watched his lips moving, but the words were lost in a sound like water surging just out of sight, an ominous imminent roar that spoke to me of the power of currents. Yes, my friends, my little boat was being drawn unstoppably forward, to that place where the river takes a suicide plunge and spectral rainbows tell their lies of beauty. Next thing I knew, Mr. Stearns was leading me from the room, down the staircase, and into that glorious dimension of light and air; and as we walked silently, side by side, the autumn leaves drifting down like giant inflamed snowflakes, a choking sound escaped from my throat. Mr. Stearns did not break his stalwart stride but gripped my shoulder with a tender firmness, while the leaves scudded and whispered, suggesting we order up some hot chocolate from the canteen and devote the rest of the morning to playing Scrabble.

It is strange to think that, in a few short days, I will be put to death for the crime of first-degree murder, a crime whose details continually elude my conscious grasp, like a firefly chased deeper and deeper into some dark wood. To be sure, the signing of my death warrant has been having a curious effect on both staff and inmates alike. Everyone is behaving quite inexplicably. One day, I am shunned like a leper; the next, the entire unit is making me gifts of bubble gum cigarettes and breaking into tear-jerking renditions of Negro spirituals. They seem to have settled down now, into a collective state of fearful paralysis. A hushed silence pervades the corridor, and a strange purple light seems to be bathing us all, as in the hours before some rapturous apocalypse. As for me, I float in a dreamlike place, trapped between doubt and belief, not unlike someone who, upon entering a funeral parlor to bid farewell to an old friend, is asked, with the utmost civility, to kindly step into the open and empty casket.

Yes.

No.

It is undeniable. It is impossible. This divided world. Do you believe, gentle reader, that for every self there is an other, a single other who is the second half of a whole, a being of uniqueness identical to one's own? That some of us meet that counterpart at an inevitable point in space and time, and fewer of us still, having found that other, lose them forever? Is there a place where that lost other waits for us, a place without jealousies or possessiveness, a place without hurting, where severed life can be rejoined? I have squandered everything.

Everything.

Tonight, I have received the correspondence that I have been eagerly awaiting. In light of my circumstances, many of you will no doubt be surprised by its nature; others, the incurable romantics in the crowd, have perhaps seen it coming from the start: the cherub's arrow tracing its invisible arc, whistling softly toward its destination and lodging in the humble breast of my diary. Without further delay, let me state that the object of my affections is most absolutely not one of my fellow prisoners. For me, eros is a thing governed by the soul, not the libido; and passion grows out of a mutual sensitivity, shared dreams, and a Frommian conception of the intimate, as opposed to the preoccupation with bodily apertures, which seems, regrettably, to be the foundation of most jailhouse homoeroticism. Breathe easy. It is not a fellow inmate of whom I speak. For even if my emotional makeup allowed for such an alliance, there is simply no future in relationships whose common denominator is a sentence of death—nothing down that road but pain and suffering. No, this affair has nothing to do with depravity and delusion. It has to do with language and love.

Even now, as I type away, she gazes at me, in wallet size, from the wall of my cell. Her auburn hair and gently freckled face. Her dark, void-like eyes, and lashes so long and majestically curved they seem to breach the two-dimensional plane of the photograph, reaching out in an undying butterfly kiss. She is not smiling so much as daring the photographer, with an airy expression, to attempt to capture the fullness of her in the corner of a middle school gymnasium. Her letter, which skated into my cell just after midnight, rests on the bed beside me. Her words are desperate, misted lightly with a cinnamon perfume, replete with superlatives, and shining with girlish fables of our alternate realities.

I wonder what is more desirable: To be the author of such a work, or the one to whom it is dedicated? To be she who seals the envelope, or he who opens it? She who lies awake in a warm bedroom, anxiously separated from the letter in question, or he who lies awake in a cold cell, in covetous possession of it? What, I wonder, is more tragic: To be condemned to love—or condemned to die? To be the teenage daughter of a warden, or to be that same warden's teenage prisoner?

It is through the kindness and courage of Mr. Stearns, the most romantic screw ever to walk the cold hallways of death row, that Francesca and I have corresponded in times of emergency and, on occasions as rare and heart-stopping as a total eclipse of the sun, have met in person, after dark, in the deserted recesses of the prison complex. Several nights after my grievous news from the governor's office, she staged a decoy sleepover at the house of a friend, and Mr. Stearns arranged for a nocturnal supply truck to smuggle her past the gate. It was dangerous business; if discovered, Mr. Stearns's correctional career would be ruined, Francesca would be shipped off to some all-girls preparatory school at the summit of a puritanical mountain, and I . . . well, what did I have left to risk? My capacity for self-sacrifice had been hunted to extinction.

Just after midnight, I heard my friend's approach, his keys jangling softly and seductively. I'd passed the evening in candlelight, reading Rilke's *Book of Hours* and staring at Francesca's photo, and was in a rather mystical frame of mind. As my cell door eased open, I laid my book down, securing the photograph tenderly between its prayers, and extinguished my candle flame. Of course, there was the usual needling from the peanut gallery. Suggestive whistling, the breathy sounds of ersatz feminine ecstasy, all broadcast at a volume low enough that we could still hear Jimmy Lee Johnson murmuring in his sleep, reciting verbatim, as he does every night in Dickensian installments, the unabridged text of his criminal-trial transcript. The execution chamber loomed before us. Inside, there is a light that never goes out, and at night a false moonbeam streams from the window and illuminates the end of the corridor. It always seems that something should happen there after dark, in that empty shining space; and sometimes I dream about it, about a man patiently standing there in a long dark overcoat, smoking, his face unseeable in the shadow of a brimmed hat. But I don't know who he is or what he is waiting for. I hugged the far wall, trying to avoid the touch of that light. Soon enough, we were safely on our way to the rendezvous point.

"I'm frightened," I whispered.

"You love her," Mr. Stearns said. "Love is two-thirds fear, kiddo."

I pressed a hand against my chest. I was half out of my body now, as Francesca, I knew, was half out of hers. Mr. Stearns stopped at the entrance to the shower room, rapped in code on the door, then inserted the key into the lock. The lock tumbled rhythmically. The door swung open and she flung her arms around my neck, pressing her wet cheek against mine. Oh, Kooky, she said, again and again. How long since our last embrace? Five months, three weeks, and four days. And now, in her arms, the endlessness of that time was burned away in a flash, as torment is burned away for the martyr, the raw fibers of his soul tingling with a glorious ascent. Mr. Stearns had withdrawn, soundlessly, into the hall. The door was closed behind us. We stood alone in the showers, before the row of animal cage stalls. I snapped off the lights and, in the pitch blackness, the tiled walls became the walls of a secret grotto, the leaky plumbing the syncopated drip of water into an underground pool. There was little to be said in words. This was farewell and both of us knew it. With each precious moment, I committed to memory another detail of her—the scent of her hair, the topography of her lips, the pitch and timbre of her voice as she repeated, in a slowly swelling crescendo, that term of endearment that is one of the three points on our triangle of love. You see, I am Kookla, she is Fran, and our first-born son, he was to be named Oliver.

My friends, it is with some difficulty that I compose this entry, the wrist of my dominant hand being sprained, sight in my left eye less than perfect, and my myriad cuts still stinging from the touch of Dr. Greiner's iodine. But a writer's work cannot be postponed on account of pain. On the contrary, there is no state more fertile for the act of composition than one of mental or physical anguish; so on with the story, which takes us now on a second journey across the prison grounds, identical to the first in all respects but that Mr. Stearns has been supplanted by Mr. Corrigan and the autumn sun by dark clouds spitting pebbles of hail all over the place. At present, the hail has turned to rain; but this morning—only hours after my tragic and transcendent conjunction with my secret love—it was hail bouncing violently off the rooftops and the walkways and off my head and face, which I protected, as best I could, with my bare shackled hands, while I was shoved and dragged forward by the temperamental and less-than-popular Mr. Corrigan. On the second floor of the small brick building, the frosty-windowed door stood open, and the warden sat at his desk in an amber glow, the giant framed photograph of the felled redwood trees spotlit by a tiny lamp affixed to the top of the frame. Without taking his bespectacled eyes off a stapled report, he nodded gravely, and Mr. Corrigan exited the room, leaving me just inside the door. The warden flipped a page. The hail tapped percussively against the building. A few cold stones lodged in my hair silently melted. He flipped another page and, as he digested its content, reached out to a small collection of picture frames that stood clustered at one corner of his desk. Very slowly, he rotated one of them, turning the image to face me. Francesca's seventh-grade photograph. I had, suddenly, an uncontrollable urge to urinate.

"Sleep well, my boy?"

Outside, the storm had lost its frigid edge, and rain was tracing lachrymal pathways down the panes of the twin windows. The warden set the report down on the desk. Removed his reading glasses and gently folded the arms together. He fixed me with a leaden stare, which elicited a warm trickle down the inner thigh of my left leg.

"Sir . . ."

"There's no need to explain, my boy. I was young once, you know." He rose to his feet and stepped slowly out from behind the desk. "It is my conviction," he said, "that the adolescent male bears no true responsibility for actions taken under the duress of passion, be it of a violent or romantic nature. What I must do to you, my boy, three days hence and in the next several minutes, runs contrary to all my personal beliefs as a social reformer. However, as I feel you well know, the private self is rarely in concert with the public. As the director of this facility, and as the father of a twelve-year-old girl, certain responsibilities, arguably unfortunate ones, fall to me, and to me alone. A man's bond with his daughter is peerless in its complication. It is fraught with horrible jealousies, unspeakable fantasies, and a loving devotion that is like a sun unto the fleeting spark of your carnal desire. Do I make myself clear, my boy?"

I nodded, shut my eyes, and a moment later felt myself propelled forward, losing my balance and careening headfirst into the side of a piece of furniture. A blood vessel had burst somewhere above the bridge of my nose. My bladder was emptied. As I struggled to my knees, I saw before me, on the edge of the desk, Francesca's tender freckled face, turned as if forced to watch these proceedings. I reached up and averted her eyes. Then I felt the warden's hands lifting me by the collar of my shirt.

Dreamed last night of a dark little house and an unkempt yard, its grass dotted with dandelions whose flowering heads were as brilliant as suns and whose souls, when I blinked, appeared in the air wherever I looked. There was a terror stealing my breath away. This thing with a door and a roof and windows. This thing that hides the secrets of its dwellers, that absorbs truth into its walls and carpets, its closets and beds. I looked down at the gun sleeping soundly in the embrace of my right hand; and for the first time, I thought to question my attitude toward it. Until now, I'd been treating it like some irreplaceable possession, holding it near, refusing release as one refuses to release a newfound lover or a talisman for fear that someone else will snatch it up and steal away its protections and its charms. But what, after all, did I know of this weapon? To be sure, we had awoken together in that dark little room in the house across the unkempt yard; in all likelihood, we had shared something there, however inaccessible the memory; and we remained, to this very minute, in each other's intimate company—and yet, the sight of it filled me with unease, for did closeness not go hand in hand with vulnerability; had I not, in all likelihood, revealed to it a measure of my deepest secrets; and might I not find myself, at some future time, betrayed by the very thing I'd trusted so completely?

There seemed little choice but to bury it in the woods.

But before I could do so, I was awakened by the sounds of morning. Locks springing open in the distance, the slow advance of the breakfast carts. A handful of prisoners stirring from sleep. Urine jetting into toilet bowls. The ignition of cigarettes. The choking infamy of Money G's morning bowel movement, making its way up the corridor with the invisible menace of biological weaponry. I went to the sink to wash my face and underarms. I noted the appearance of yet another curling hair in the center of my breastbone. There are five now. Five little black weeds growing in the center of my chest. Then I turned to see the warden and several guards passing by my cell, carrying a small, darkly varnished wooden booster seat, reminiscent of those encountered in one's friendly neighborhood barbershop, and a crudely fashioned mannequin of youthful stature. I must say, it is difficult to subdue one's curiosity under such circumstances. Your impulse, I can tell you, is to take your little mirror from the edge of the sink and, easing it through the bars of your cell, angle its reflective surface in a westerly direction, that direction where the sun is wont to set and the day to come to a close. Having myself obeyed this impulse, I was able to see that blank-faced sexless doll—limp wrists and ankles strapped and a metal halo embracing its head—sitting placidly in the large oaken chair.

It was quite some time later that I emerged from darkness, a sharp pain at the back of my head. Evidently, I had lost consciousness and pitched backward, striking the top of my typewriter. Since the signing of my death warrant, these blackouts have become increasingly frequent. I must remember to speak to Dr. Greiner. A writer such as I, one who relies on autobiography as the foundation of his art, simply cannot be fainting at the slightest provocation. By the time I got back to the bars and reinstated my view of the corridor's end, the execution room door was shut, and my powdered eggs had grown cold, a family of houseflies busy on the jaundiced surface, like pioneers who have pushed west and claimed partial ownership of a dream.

Earlier this afternoon, I received a phone call from my young and idealistic attorney. I have not seen much of her of late. She has had little time for social visits, frantic as she has been with her eleventh-hour attempts to save my life. At the booth, in the shadow of Mr. Corrigan, I took the phone (somewhat nervously, I must admit) in my two cuffed hands and held it to my ear. The famed metropolitan firm had placed me on hold and was transmitting a piece of classical music—the first aggrieved movement, if

I am not mistaken, of Saint-Saëns's Symphony no. 3 in C Minor, a composition that spoke to me of denied appeals and rejected pleas for executive clemency. I imagined my beautiful and idealistic attorney sitting at her desk, countless stories above the teeming city, staring at her telephone and the little red light throbbing on it like a heart. Abruptly the music disappeared, the vacated space filled by the sound of a woman crying.

"Liza?"

"I'm a failure," she sobbed.

I twisted the phone cord around my fingers. Her sadness was like a tropical storm raging in some distant latitude.

"It was unanimous," she said. "Seven to none. Not even one dissent."

"Well," I said, after a long and awkward silence, "law isn't everything," at which she burst again into tears, choking and wheezing, everything muffled as if she were trying to suffocate herself in the plush leather of her office chair.

"He left me yesterday," she said.

I burrowed deeper into the corner of the booth. I tried to hide from Mr. Corrigan as I extended a pinky and cleared a strange and disconcerting wetness from my cheek.

"Billy left me," she repeated, "for an aerobics instructor."

Considering all that has happened recently, it came as no small surprise that the warden had designated my final meeting with my biological mother a contact visit. Instead of sitting on opposite sides of the glass wall, in a silence punctuated by occasional commas and semicolons of speech, we converged in a small room furnished with a faux-leather couch, an end table with a plastic ashtray, and a television hanging ominously, like a giant wasps' nest, from one corner of the ceiling. She drew me into her spongy mass, arms clamping around me, then held me by the shoulders and stared at me intently, like a schoolgirl straining to memorize the spelling of some strange and multisyllabic vocabulary word. We were supplied with junk food, soda, and coffee. My mother smoked her mentholated cigarettes while we watched reruns of situation comedies, avoiding news magazines, live broadcasts, and monologues of late-night talk shows, whose jokes were centered around tomorrow's historic event. Finally, she commenced shifting in her seat, making the frictional motions of the guest who wishes to be released from social enslavement. I told her I had to be getting back to the deathwatch cell, I still had some important entries to record in my diary; and she said they'd be missing her outside the gate, at the candlelight vigil. She did not kiss me goodbye, but how can I blame her? The events of these last few years have put my poor biological family through a battery of tests that few could hope to pass. We, if I may employ that cozy pronoun, have been torn asunder. Suffice it to say that even now, as I type away, my mother stands beyond the prison's northern wall, holding her tiny waxen torch under the black canopy of night, singing hymns with the advocates of mercy, while my father, in his smoky rented room, prepares his statements for the press on the morality of retribution and the demands of justice.

Gentle mother and angry father.

But let me not misrepresent, let me not oversimplify either one of them. My mother, I know, despises me, regrets the day I exited, breathing, from her womb; and my father, I am certain, feels the deathly pain of Abraham, and even as he lashes me to the rock and raises the dagger over my heart, he is waiting for a voice to call out from above and release him from his duty. What will happen to them after I am gone? The strange weather of love cannot be forecast, for often does the sun not shine in one chamber of the heart even as the other floods with rain? I want to believe that after this affair concludes itself, my mother and father will find their way back to each other, to a place uncomplicated by children, and live out the rest of their days in peace. The greater part of me, though, the part that has given up the reading of fairy tales, fears that cozy pronouns no longer have a place in our lexicon of thought and speech, that like the particles of a split atom we are spinning hopelessly, randomly through space, and that a conflict of this kind can find its end only in divorce.

Soon, very soon, the film version of this sad and stormy saga will be featured at your local multiplex, and you will learn all the details that I cannot supply. On this very night, even as I type, the film is enjoying its premiere at the famous Chinese Theatre in the City of Angels. Yes, the premiere is tonight; and I regret to say that—despite a gracious invitation that even now, from the wall of my cell, requests the pleasure of my company at this gala event—I am not in attendance, as I have a prior engagement at dawn sharp. Earlier today, I was quite upset about this conflict. Quite childishly upset. I spent hours sulking on my cot, refusing to eat, refusing to speak or communicate in any way. At high noon, under the general heading of protest and rebellion, I urinated through the bars of my cell and into the corridor, and a few hours later, on the way to the shower, threw a temper tantrum so violently irrational that it was necessary to sedate me for my own safety. Since then, I have come to accept the hard, if somewhat obvious, fact that in this life one often encounters obstacles immune to the power of desire.

So.

I am not in the audience on this thrilling night; I am not standing by, tuxedoed and discreetly handcuffed, while the film's young star, my cinematic double, presses his hands into the primordial sludge of that famous sidewalk; and I am not being chauffeured afterwards to the private party at his Malibu beach house. I can see it, though, blurry and silent in the crystal ball of my imagination. An amoeba-shaped swimming pool, its water slick with varicolored reflections. Blue-noted jazz winding through the air. Celebrities born from the pages of shiny magazines and tabloid newspapers. Tipsy on sparkling cider, my auburn-haired consort and truest love has plotted our intimate escape from the madding crowd. Down the cliffside we go, my hands, with sudden magician's skill, slipping free of their binding. The moon like fresh milk spilled all over the surface of the ocean. The waves making love with the beach while we run barefoot, she and I, falling to the sand. Surf washing against us as we kiss. Wet salt, the smell of freedom filling my lungs, as the thwap thwap thwap of a helicopter becomes audible. Searchlights sweep the beach, illuminating momentarily a group of armed men who are moving, with the lanky lope of wolves, over the sandy terrain. Sirens wailing from the heights. A bullhorned voice demanding my peaceful surrender. Do I have any final words? I was a killer once; now I am a writer.

DESTROY ALL MONSTERS

Haruo Nakajima/Monster Zero

Monster Zero swept, swooped, as if on wires suspended from the roof of the cosmos, over the dead horizon of Planet X. Fuck these aliens in their shiny jumpsuits, whoever the fuck they were, out here on the blind side of Jupiter. Made no difference who had been here first. What was *first*? — indigenous was one thing, but *first* — and even indigenous (now that his middle head, the most cerebral of the three, came to think of it) had a spurious ring to it, because there was always something before, always something earlier than the now, before humanoids, even before kaiju like himself, who'd been lurking in oceanic trenches or nesting inside dormant volcanoes or trapped in hurtling meteors for millennia unknown, who knew how long, but a hell of a lot longer than there'd been any anthropoids stumbling toward pathetic notions of spiritual and technological fruition. Now he felt the fire in his fangs, now tasted the sweetness of it on his forked tongues; and a moment later a triad of gravity beams, crackling threads of electromagnetism, bolted from his three maws. No gravity beams, of course (beams later, animation department)—but as he swooped over the sound stage, Nakajima couldn't help but notice: no pyrotechnics either. What the fuck. Plastic explosives were supposed to be going off in three separate directions (corresponding to the distinct angles of his heads) along the surface of the miniature planet, throwing up great clouds of plaster dust and jolting the underground tunnels and command centers of slit-eyed space invaders—but Nakajima, inside Monster Zero, in the triple-digit heat of the synthetic rubber suit, could not hear any moon rock blowing sky high; only the boss blowing his top. Cut! Cut! Just like that, the take, the attack, was over. Someone had screwed up down there. Some puny assistant too incompetent to light a goddamn fuse. I'll electromagnetize him, thought Monster Zero. It was the kind of idea that always originated in the head that was right of center: the angry head, the head that was never happy unless anthropoids were being terrorized and famous landmarks were being smashed to smithereens and so-called civilization was generally going up in flames; and even then, even when it all finally came together in postproduction, even as the effects departments inked the gravity beams and synched the demoniacal shrieks, already Monster Zero would be feeling the return of a rage that could only be slaked by another surprise attack. Sometimes the middle head had to wonder. As for the other one, the left one, strange waves came from the brain in that head. A Toho Company–American International Pictures Production. Hiroshima. Nagasaki. And the nominees for Best Actor in a Supporting Role are . . . Nick Adams, *Twilight of Honor*. 1964.

Miriam Schumann

Nick Adams. Nick Adams. Miriam had tried to think. The name did not ring a bell. The headshots—of a man with blond hair slicked back in a wave, not handsome exactly, but attractive, a wholesome face, an amiable smile, a boy in a man's body—had not looked familiar. The director, Ishiro Honda, had told her the American had been nominated the year prior for an Academy Award. She had not heard of the film. The day he arrived, in a Hawaiian print shirt and sunglasses, she met him at the airport. The chauffeur took Mr. Adams's suitcase and Mr. Adams took Miriam's arm. Call me Nick. She had been told to impress the honored guest with a tour of the metropolis. So they drove on the new Expressway Number 4 and saw Tokyo Tower and wound up trapped in the madness of downtown at midday. An entanglement of automobiles and trolley cars and pedestrians, highway overpasses and elevated tracks, air hammers slamming rivets, jet planes on approach and departure. At Sukiyabashi, the electronic billboard read eighty-three decibels, then eighty-four . . .

Mr. Adams—

Nick.

Alright. Nick. Is Los Angeles very busy, too?

He gave her that winning smile and said: Miriam, LA is Sleepville compared to this cuckoo place.

Nick Adams/Astronaut Glenn

Tokyo.

Never in his life—thirty-four years and counting—had Nick imagined he'd find himself here. He had sworn, in fact, in more than one interview with more than one hack columnist, that he'd never make a picture overseas. But here he was, in Japan of all places. To pilot the flagship rocket ship of the United Space Nations, the United Nations of Space, something like that, to a strange new planet. Of which he knew next to nothing. Because he had not read the script. "You're an astronaut," his agent had told him a year earlier, over gin martinis at Romanoff's. "There's giant monsters in the picture, too. One has three heads." A giant three-headed monster, Nick had thought, surveying the joint, eyes smarting just a little. He had to take a leak, and set down on the bar his stemmed glass and set sail for the men's room; and that's where he was, streaming piss into a pure white porcelain basin, when Marlon Brando appeared beside him, unzipping, unpacking the penis of a thoroughbred horse.

Who are you, Brando said.

Nick Adams.

Don't wink at another man when he's urinating.

I don't.

Only Maoists and repressed homosexuals wink at urinating men.

Oh, I'm not queer, Nick said.

Brando didn't seem to hear. He had tilted his head up, closed his eyes as if to begin a heavenly ascent. Nick stole another glance before tamping his own average member into his trousers. Brando pissed: a torrent of piss, like hydroelectric outflow. Nick flushed and went to the sink. Washed his hands. Put the wave of his blond hair back in place. Now what? Keep talking. Ask him if he saw the picture. Courtroom drama, poor sap on trial. That was me. Maybe you saw the ads in the trades. Maybe you were at the Oscars. But Nick didn't say anything else to Brando that day. He fled. Fled to the bar. Willson, still there. Pinching a toothpick between thumb and forefinger, sucking Tanqueray off an impaled green olive. Nick wanted to clock him. Right there in the middle of Romanoff's. Three punches in his fag nose, one for each head of the goddamn monster who was out there in the shadows of the solar system, hiding, waiting for Astronaut Glenn.

❧

Willson had told him where to go. The Shinjuku District. A neighborhood called Nicho. But Nick was beat, jet-lagged; and in the morning, he had to meet Honda at Toho. He went to the hotel lounge and discovered the bartender was American. Grew up in Newark. No kidding, Nick said. I'm from Jersey City. Audobon Park. He drank highballs and confessed. He was in Tokyo to do a monster picture. Finally, around midnight, the concierge came looking for him. Telephone, Adams-san. She pointed him in the direction of the house phone. What time was it in the States? He couldn't do the math. Probably Saperstein. Maybe Willson. Wondering if he'd found the baths. Nick picked up the phone.

Hello.

Guess what I'm doing, said his wife after an awkward long-distance delay.

What are you doing.

Fucking.

He hung up and placed a twenty on the bar and wandered the floors of the hotel trying to find his suite. Finally, he recalled the key in his pocket with the number printed on it. He scheduled a wake-up for seven and took a promazine and fell asleep in the same clothes he'd worn for the crossing.

Miriam Schumann

In the morning, Miriam was fifteen minutes early, and Nick was half an hour late. She sat by the big window of Mr. Honda's office that looked out over the back lot of Toho, reading the English translation of the shooting script. *The Great Monster War*. She had never seen one of these movies: kaiju eiga. She knew about them, of course. They were very popular here. But she had never felt the slightest urge to buy a ticket and watch one. Not that she wasn't interested in cinema. She saw every Kurosawa film. Sometimes she even went to American movies. John Wayne, Grace Kelly, Marlon Brando speaking in hyōjungo. She knew other expats who found the effect humorous. Miriam couldn't stand it. Given a choice, however, she would take the phoniness of dubbed dialogue over the total inanity of giant monsters fighting a war in outer space.

Honda-san, Adams-san has arrived. Mr. Honda flipped a switch on the intercom and instructed the secretary to show the American in immediately. The heavy door opened; and as soon as Nick appeared on the threshold, Miriam could feel color coming into her cheeks. How maddening. Blushing over what? Mr. Honda stood up. Miriam braced for the usual confusion. The Easterner would bow and the Westerner would almost poke his eyes out trying to shake hands. But the two men walked right up to one another and successfully introduced themselves.

Konnichiwa, Honda-san.

Konnichiwa, Adams-san.

Morning, Miriam.

Good morning, Mr. Adams. I mean, Nick.

Next came questions and answers about the trip, the accommodations. Each time one man spoke, the other looked to Miriam for the translation. Then Mr. Honda invited Nick to join him at the conference table on the other side of the office; and again, as he had yesterday at the airport, Nick took Miriam by the arm. And he pulled out a chair for her. Smelling very strongly. Of soap.

Eiji Tsuburaya/Visual Effects

Tsuburaya Eiji, towering over the Chiyoda Ward in his suit jacket, dark glasses, and fedora, forgot for a moment about Monster Zero and remembered how, on that March night in 1945 (a year after Hajime had been born and a few months shy of Hiroshima and Nagasaki and, at long last, after too long, the end)—how he, Eiji, with all the might of his forty-four years, had prayed silently to his wife's god, praying, even as he told his elder son in a voice strong and sure the tale about Sir Old Man Who Makes Trees Blossom, that the American bombs miss them; or that they, his family, pass somehow unburned through the fire. Kami-sama,

Kami-sama! Honda-san is on his way with the American! Tsuburaya calmly removed cigarettes from the lining of his jacket. He knew very well that Honda was on his way with the American. The time was 10:25. They were to arrive at half past. Why must production assistants constantly state the obvious? And call him by that ridiculous honorific? He continued his inspection of the set. Everything looked good. Then he noticed the automobiles across from the Diet Building. Not arranged realistically. He put a cigarette in his mouth. Held it ready between his lips while he went to one knee and disturbed the uniform order of the automobiles by shifting one a few millimeters this way, another a few millimeters that way.

There.

Now his Tokyo was ready to be brought down. Tsuburaya stepped off the set and lit his cigarette. Pacing while the cameramen took their light readings and the wire operators checked their knots and Nakajima changed into Monster Zero. They had done this before, he and Nakajima. The first time, Nakajima had attacked as the fire-breathing sea creature; the second, as the supersonic pteranodon. Today, he would attack as the three-headed space dragon. And the American would be watching. Nick Adams. Tsuburaya had not heard of him. Of course, he had seen *Rebel Without a Cause*. A film which had moved and disturbed him. But Adams's part as a teenage villain had been very small. If the young actor had made any impression, it had not been a deep one. Recently, Adams had come close to a high honor in the States. An Academy Award. He had not won. But Tsuburaya fully expected him to behave as if he had, as if a single brush with acclaim conferred godhood. And what will the man know of me? Of any of us? Nothing. Of that Tsuburaya was quite certain. No matter. The American would be Honda's headache. Tsuburaya had his own concerns. Eight wires, four operators, three cameras shooting in tandem. Nakajima from the northeast, wings flapping, heads lashing. Signal Kobori to trip detonator one and your lovingly created world will come apart, buildings bursting, plaster dust rising, kerosene-soaked rags catching fire so Tokyo may burn again as it did that night when the B-29s came from the South Seas and for six hours Masano held and nursed the panicking infant and you told Akira one tale after another, secretly praying, outwardly gagging on the windborne flatus of burning gasoline and poison gas and what you knew to be the char of human bodies, your mind insisting all the while on one word: monsters, monsters. Tsuburaya had finished the cigarette. Kami-sama, Kami-sama! Look, the American is here!

Nick Adams/Astronaut Glenn

Willson's directions: get into a cab and say Shinjuku. And just as Willson had foretold, the driver grinned at Nick and delivered him to a nexus of streets ablaze with sex: with neon and girls, black haired, pale skinned, calling out from curtained doorways. It had been raining. The streets were wet. Each car, in passing, sounded to Nick like a wave on a beach, heard through lidded eyes under the narcosis of summer sun, as in those days—1946, 1947, the Jersey Shore: Point Pleasant, Avalon, Ocean City—days when there were only girls. Places he'd not been back to, and to which he knew he would never return. He belonged to a different ocean now, to the coastline of the saints: Santa Monica, San Buenaventura, Santa Barbara. He belonged to Henry Willson. The prick. As he walked past exotic dancers and peep shows, under foreign signage and the reflections of it in darkened windows, Nick wondered who was more contemptible: his prick of an agent or his slut of a wife.
Hello.
Guess what I'm doing, she'd said.
Fucking.

No. Filing for divorce. I've got the papers right here in front of me. I get the house, Nick. I'm going to live here with Ally and Jeb. And don't you dare try to do a goddamn thing about it.

Carol. Hey. Hello.

She had hung up, or they'd been disconnected. Either way, Nick had stood there, in the hinterlands of the hotel lobby, holding the phone, as if the call were not over, though he knew perfectly well it was over. Midnight now. In the sleazy groin of a weird city. Trying to find someone. But where? Nick felt dizzy. Shouldn't have had that second drink, shouldn't have taken a pill in the taxi. The way he found the place was the way you find places in dreams. Suddenly: tiled floors, pools of water, welcoming steam. Nick had been to all the ones in Los Angeles. Pico, Gemini, the Palace. That's where he'd gotten his break. A balding chinless man with a pickle for a cock. Henry Willson. He looked like a child molester. He was actually a talent agent.

Konbanwa.

It sounded like a greeting. Certainly, the boy's eyes were friendly. Body perfectly hairless, an abdomen like the membrane of a drum. Nick took his hand and walked deeper into the warm mist.

Miriam Schumann

The next morning, Miriam was the late one. She had taken too long dressing, cursing her dowdy clothes, the drab sweaters and skirts interred in the antique wardrobe that had been her mother's in the old house in Denenchofu. Then it was too late for a trolley. She would have to take the subway. At the Shibuya stop, she allowed herself to be pressed by a white-gloved attendant into the hot crush of an overcrowded car; and no sooner did the train move than a hand began to feel her breasts. Miriam could not see the man. Didn't want to. Try to think of something else. Of Kyoto. The mountains in autumn. A temple overarched by the changed leaves of maples.

From Yurakucho station she ran to Toho. Not watching as she crossed the lobby of the studio (rather, looking in her briefcase for the shooting script, for the day's xerographed scenes), she walked into him: a custodian in a gray jumpsuit, grotesquely scarred on his face, scalp, and neck. She had knocked the broom from his hands. Sumimasen, she said, bowing; the accident had been her fault alone. But the poor man would not stop apologizing in the most formal manner. He'd seemed very old at first, but now, as he snatched up his gray cap and covered his head, bowing and bowing again, Miriam could see that he wasn't much older than she and that the scars, red and crustaceous, were those of a burn victim, a bomb victim. Sumimasen, she repeated, moving away now. To the gate. Onto the lot. Breathing heavily. From the run. And from the shock of seeing the man, and colliding with him. A hibakusha. Yoshiko had taught her that word, a word for those who had been in Hiroshima or Nagasaki—and lived. The custodian was one of them.

Up ahead: the wardrobe department. Costumed actors clustered outside, laughing and gesticulating. Nick was at the center of the group in an orange astronaut flight suit, a huge smile on his face.

Miriam, he said, waving to her.

I'm late.

Don't sweat it. I'd like you to meet some people. Astronaut Fuji, the King of Planet X, and Miss Namikama.

The first man was dressed just like Nick. The other man and the woman, whom Miriam understood to be playing the parts of alien invaders, wore silver uniforms that gave them the look of futuristic fencers. They introduced themselves, but Miriam didn't seem to hear the names. Her mind still on the accident in the lobby, her mind working like a counting machine, estimating the man to be thirty, thirty-five, making him ten or fifteen in August of 1945, when she, a girl of eleven, had come from the wet heat of a New England summer into the shade-drawn afternoon of the parlor to find her mother sobbing over the armchair radio from which a voice was announcing that the war was over, finally over. Six months later: New York to California, California to Hawaii, Hawaii to Tokyo. Her father, a man from a dream in a khaki uniform, waiting for them on the tarmac, embracing her desperately—and then, on the way to the house, forewarning her: Boys and girls, Miri; orphans, some younger than you, living on the streets; and men, soldiers turned beggars, missing parts . . . In the coming months, when walking to the market with Yoshiko, Miriam would bring candies for the children and coins for the men, though Yoshiko disapproved of the practice. No, Miri-chan. But why *not*, Yoshi? For a long time, for months, there was one boy in particular, always begging in the same place: on a street corner near the market, by a pole with kanji characters painted on it and appended with a sign that read in Roman letters, TIMES SQUARE. Every time she saw the boy, Miri couldn't look, yet couldn't look away. What had happened to him? Yoshiko refused to explain. Then, one day, she finally explained; and then, one day, the boy was gone. Now, they were all laughing, whoever they really were. Astronaut Fuji and the King of Planet X and Miss Namikama. Nick was doing an impression of someone, a famous American actor. It was spot on, but Miriam couldn't think of the name.

Ishiro Honda/Direction

That evening, Honda met up with Kurosawa. A few blocks from the studio, at an izakaya that Kurosawa said made the best skewered chicken in the city. Honda did not agree. But then he was not an expert on skewered chicken. It was spring, the cherry trees blooming, a sweetness in the air when the petals stirred on the trees and fell to earth, making Honda think of corny songs from the war. Up and down the street, hanging lanterns glowed in the dusk like the hives of radioactive bees.

Ino-chan.

Kurosawa had already ordered the sake and consumed more than his share of the bottle. Now he poured out a cup for Honda.

Cheers, Ino-chan.

Cheers, said Honda, sitting down and taking a sip. Kurosawa drained his own cup and poured himself another. Honda's old friend was drinking again. In the old days, before the war, it was beer near Shibuya Station, sake with dinner, then on to the Ginza bars for whiskey. Back then, they were boys, getting drunk to speak in tongues about movies, projecting onto a screen of shared imagination all the films of their dreams—and not in the wildest of them did Honda see monsters coming from the sea and air to raze and burn. It was never his dream. He came back from the war and made a war picture. The kaiju—that was Tsuburaya's idea. Now, after nine movies going on ten, the monsters were like Honda's adopted children. Kurosawa finished the first bottle of sake and ordered a second with the food and started complaining about his shoot, a bit player named Sada, whom the master had found it necessary to scold to the verge of tears. Kuro-chan didn't get along with any actor but Mifune, which recalled for Honda how well he'd gotten on all day with the American. Admittedly, Honda had been apprehensive at first: a coproduction with a foreign actor he'd never met much less auditioned—never in a million years would Kuro-chan agree to such an arrangement. But Adams had been easy to direct. Moreover, everyone had taken an immediate liking to him.

Incidentally, Kurosawa said, I saw your American today.

Adams.

He waved at me. He was waving at everyone on the lot in that absurd costume, as if he really just had returned from the moon.

You mean, Planet X. You see, Kuro-chan, there is a mysterious planet on the far side of Jupiter—

Ino-chan . . .

And the space dragon with three heads —

Ino-chan, spare me. Your story lines aggravate my ulcers.

Honda smiled and chewed his soybeans. Once upon a time, that twist of derision in Kuro-chan's voice could hurt his feelings. But as every passing year took him a little deeper into his fifties, Honda felt an ease, a contentment he'd thought would always evade him. Strange now to think of the heartache and the harpings of that inner voice. Why can't you be Kurosawa? The answer turned out to be simple. Because you are Honda. Not a visionary; not a master. Merely the friend of one.

Nick Adams/Astronaut Glenn

The divorce papers arrived by airmail. All that day, Nick had been beneath the surface of Planet X, shooting scenes with the alien controller, a hell of a good guy named Tsuchiya, who had been in every Kurosawa picture since *Rashomon* and cracked everyone up with impersonations of Marlon Brando. Around five, they wrapped for the day. As Nick walked across the lot, cherry trees in flower made him think of the boy from the baths, and a spike of feeling nearly doubled him over. Needed a pill. Was he taking too many? One upon waking and another upon going to sleep; one to get into and another to get out of character. Starting to lose count. He opened the door of his dressing room. The envelope had been slipped underneath. NICK ADAMS C/O TOHO STUDIOS. Though it was the middle of the night in Los Angeles, he placed the call. United States, Oleander-653.

Hello?

Carol. Listen.

Nick?

There's a movie in London. Right after this one. You could go over with Ally and Jeb. I'll take you to Paris on the weekends. Then after the shoot . . .

He couldn't understand his own self. Even Honda, Tsuchiya, all these strange kind people made more sense to Nick than Nick Adams, who was wearing an orange astronaut costume on a movie studio in Tokyo asking his harpy wife to join him in England while he did another B-list picture for that Shylock, Saperstein. Horror picture with Karloff. Spooky mansion. Some sort of curse. Monsters in the greenhouse. Nick must have fallen asleep. Holding the divorce papers and the telephone. Now he was dreaming. Of darkness. And suffocating heat. Buried alive, he guessed. Closed up in a coffin that felt like a second skin. He could hear people on the outside. Astronaut Fuji, Tsuchiya. All gibberish. But another voice, too—female and comforting. Translating. He's in there. Get him out. Don't let him die like this. But Nick knew it was already too late. He had passed on a long time ago, when that loopy son of a bitch, a veteran of the Pacific War, had picked him up in Las Vegas and driven him to Los Angeles through Death Valley in the high noon of summer 1948. Nick could not remember the man's face, but the voice was undying, unchangeable, like narration from a great beyond. You think this is hell. Believe me, kid. This is not hell.

Miriam Schumann

Miriam couldn't make sense of the story. Every day, she received new pages of the script—Nick's scenes for the following day—but not in proper order. First, they did pages 25–35 on a set at Toho. Then they caravanned to Hokkaido to shoot the final scene on a cliff above the Sea of Japan (Glenn and Fuji in civilian clothes, reacting to a climactic brawl of monsters yet to be staged in miniature by the effects director), then back to Tokyo and the astronaut costumes, back to the very beginning, the rocket ship and the strange planet in the shadow of Jupiter. She wasn't sure how it would all coherently fit together. How *could* the sum be coherent when each part was so nonsensical? One night, at a cocktail party at Mr. Honda's country house, Miriam had a little too much sake, and she said to Nick:

Isn't it funny.

What?

The movie. The dialogue and the plot. Everything . . .

He flinched at her words. Alone in the garden, cherry trees arching over them, a full moon, her view of things afloat on gentle swells. Miriam Schumann kept, and would always keep, one memento from the war. A girl's tea set stamped OCCUPIED JAPAN. Expressions of surrender. For years, she had read them on the faces of orphaned children, maimed soldiers, drivers, and maids, even in the eyes of officials who'd entered the house as honored guests. Somehow, that night in the garden, she failed to see that Nick had been defeated, too. She thought he felt insulted. To make amends, she said very brightly:

Oh, I've been talking with a fan of yours.

She pretty?

Not a girl. A man. He knows you from a western. American westerns were very big here—he says yours was the best.

That's nice to know.

He works at the studio. As a custodian . . .

Miriam wanted to tell Nick the whole story. How she'd collided with the man in the lobby and then a few days later saw him again, same gray jumpsuit and cap, broom and dustpan, again her throat clogging with guilt; and when he called—misu, misu—she pretended not to hear. What could he possibly want from her? What could she ever say? Misu, he repeated. This belongs to you. Holding something between two burned and palsied fingers. A brooch, a piece of costume jewelry.

What's his name? Nick asked.

Mikio.

Miriam watched Nick turning a cherry blossom over in his hand, the flower glowing faintly in the moonlight, the garden embowered with flowers and faintly glowing. He's a hibakusha, she finally said—and then explained the meaning of the word.

Mikio Tanaka/Hibakusha

The season ended. Now white petals lay all around, like ash fall. Not near his tenement home under the gray-green smog of the port, but in the parks of different wards and in the back lot of the studio. Mikio swept the dead flowers from the walkways and remembered the ash of Nagasaki. For him, a clear blue sky would always be the sky of that morning. Any plane overhead, that plane. Yes, he had heard it. On an errand by bicycle, and while returning, the river flowing at his right side, he heard the sound. Like a fly in a bottle. Must be very high up. He looked, bicycle swerving on the dirt road. Clear blue day; morning sun crowning Mount Kompira. For some reason, he rang the bell on his handlebars, as if to say, "Here I am." Then the entire city fainted—

Mikio-san.

He looked up from the heap of petals. Miriam-san, of course. The only one here who calls me by my given name. And with her: the American. How many actors had Mikio seen in his years as a kozukai? It was only natural that none of them should say good morning or wave hello to a man like himself. More monster than man. But twice in these weeks had the American star waved to him from a distance; and now here he was, walking toward Mikio, looking at him directly, looking at him. So ashamed Mikio felt, like a gray ghost of himself about to fall into white silence, as the city had that day—fainting, falling—and yet even when the atomic wind reached him and blew him and his bicycle off the ground, even as he somersaulted backward through the air like a circus acrobat, and the bicycle left his hands and feet, still his legs turned invisible gears as in a dream of bicycling, and seemed still, even now, as the American offered his hand, to be turning them. Konnichiwa, the American said. To moushimasu Nick Adams.

AD 1968

Hurtling back to Earth in the future year 1999, Monster Zero remembers the American. There is a photograph of the three of them—Adams, the woman translator whose name Monster Zero cannot recall, and himself—taken back in 1964 on Planet X. In the photo (still displayed in Nakajima's dressing room at Toho), the American looks very happy with his boyish smile and his arm around the long rubbery neck of Monster Zero's middle head. The middle head remembers Adams fondly. Sad now to hear of his death.

Only thirty-six.

How frail and short the lives of humans. How final their ends. But the space dragon has more pressing concerns than the accidental suicide of one puny anthropoid. On Earth, the century is turning and the shit storm is on. The radioactive kaiju are loose. The lizard and the pteranodon and the pupal moth et cetera. All of them. And closed up in the hot sarcophagus of the monster, swooping through the cosmos like a puppet on piano wire (no cosmos, of course; cosmos later, effects department), the man feels a terror spreading through him, equal parts remembrance and premonition: a memory of things to come.

SLEEPER WAVE

A siren, a sea-maid. Lying in the sand, slick with salt water. Wet and willing and half-human in the tide at sunset. That's the photo she e-mails him after they've been doing erotic chat for a couple of weeks. Blake has seen two pictures already. On her member page. A close-up of her face and a wider view of her naked upper half. But this third one. Taken on a beach in gentle fiery light. Auburn hair on the verge of combusting; breasts that appear to be made of soft gold; and a lower body composed of what she will later refer to as a caudal peduncle and fin. The idea has been suggested from the start. Her screen name is Lorelei. She's been claiming all along to be a mermaid. Still, this goes too far, doesn't it? This doctored image. Upsets some delicate balance of reality and fantasy. Blake isn't sure how to react. Is the girl joking? If she's sincerely trying to turn him on, should he admit it's working? One night, they're online, and he writes something about touching her inner thighs and spreading her legs.

You know I don't have legs.

No legs?

No.

Oh, right. I forgot. You're a mythical creature.

There's a long delay, and in the midnight silence he thinks he hears a noise from the other end of the house, so he minimizes the screen and pads back to the bedroom. His wife and baby are asleep together on the mattress. Back at the computer, a long reply awaits him. The tone is angry. He can tell, also, she is hurt. As if he's mocked some aspect of her in which she takes a wavering pride. She's signing off now. If you don't want to believe me, she writes, I can find about a hundred other guys who will.

The next morning, driving the baby to day care, his eyesight seems too sharp. The day is like a perfectly exposed photograph of itself. He slows for a stoplight. Sun warms the car. His daughter, not yet a year old, silent in the backward-facing seat. Blake shuts his eyes, hard. What is he doing? What was he thinking when he filled out the membership questionnaire? He can't say he didn't conceive of an affair; but he certainly had no expectation, no real intention, of starting one. He was just curious. Simply wanted to talk to someone. If he'd had a cheater's agenda, he would've lied on the questionnaire instead of admitting the truth. Married with a child. Under six feet tall and of average endowment. He wasn't looking for a relationship or no-strings sex. He just wanted to see, just wanted to know.

Now, as he waits for the light to change, his mind dreams of abandoning his family. He hasn't even met her face-to-face. Yet being with her forever seems possible to him, even necessary. He's only thirty-four! Not young, he'll admit, but too young for the kind of life he is falling into. A sexless one that makes him think of his parents' marriage. He refuses to go that quietly. As he holds the car still, he turns to check on the baby and finds her head straining in his direction, eyes as bright and clear as the world outside. His little girl! If only he could say, honestly and ardently, that he loves her. That he'd do anything for her. Make any sacrifice. Isn't that what fathers are supposed to know in their hearts? These discordant moments, these failures of feeling, come too often. Blake feels like he can't take one more of them. Can't stand to find one more flaw in himself. How can he go through the rest of life trying unsuccessfully to be a good father? He gives the baby a sympathetic smile and gets the horn from the car behind him.

We all go a little crazy sometimes. He can't remember who said that (some old-time comedian or classic cartoon character), but the words have always been in his head, one of those phrases that hook you when you're little and over time gain the weight of universal truth. The craziness took root when his wife became pregnant. He'd known her for six years; they'd been married for one. In all that time, Blake had almost never failed to feel electricity branching through him at the closeness of her body. With the evolution of the baby, he felt mainly discomfort. He can recall, with perfect clarity, how a sense of indecency had started creeping into their bed as soon as Katie really began to show, once he could no longer deny there was something living inside her. It was right there. He was either pressing on it or poking at it or staring it in the face so to speak. A typical conversation from those days held in the nude:

I'm worried I'll crush it.

She's not an it.

Her.

And you won't crush her, Blake. Oh!

She moved.

Of course she moved. Look.

And he did. He looked at his wife's belly and saw the baby (a hand, a foot) pushing against the inside of the womb, as if to test its resiliency. It was awake. It was right *there*. Sex had taken on an undertone of incest. That's when he started to understand the change coming over them. They weren't lovers anymore. They were a family.

The thing is, she's the one who contacted *him*. She sent him a "wink." One night he logged on—and there was her screen name and a link to her profile. She was eighteen. From a town he'd never heard of up the coast. Two hundred thirty-five miles away (according to the website's calculations). Her intro line read: YOUNG SEA-MAID, LOOKIN FOR SEX. Body type: slim/ petite. Education: rather not say. Sexual orientation: curious. Bra size: 34B. Looking for: men, women, couples (man and woman), couples (two women) for erotic chat or e-mail, discreet relation-ship, no-strings sex, group sex, or other "alternative" activities. In the profile, she said she needed someone open-minded and experienced. Age, race, and marital status didn't matter. She wasn't picky in the looks department. She just wanted to be satisfied and return that satisfaction. If you think you fit the bill, drop me a line. He clicked on her head shot and got a larger image. He clicked on the other picture, the one where she was topless. There came a pain in his chest, like a fishing line had been cast out across the Internet, the hook catching in his heart, the line drawn suddenly taut.

It seemed like the perfect solution. No bodies, no touching. Just text on a screen. Nothing but letters and symbols. There was really no infraction here. In a way, you could view it as a healthy outlet. Blake had decided, without much debate, that he would be a receiver only, not a sender. He'd see who winked at him and maybe he'd wink back and that would be the end of it. Now, two months later, it's absurd, but he's convinced he's falling in love. On more than one occasion, in the moments after they've come together, when they seem to be drifting, together and totally alone, in the middle of a becalmed ocean—more than once, he has almost typed those words. The idea scares him shitless. Christ, he's a father! Just a few weeks before his daughter's first birthday, and all he can think about is this gorgeous creature whose real name he doesn't even know.

Lori.

Mmm?

I want to tell you something.

It's very late, nearly two in the morning. She's just had two orgasms and now they're lying next to each other in bed, and she's holding his head to her breast and stroking his forehead. Of course, they're not really in bed. They're sitting at computer screens separated by two hundred miles. But Blake is getting used to this virtual world. His powers of imagination are improving. There are times, like tonight, when this sex seems more real, more meaningful, than anything else.

She says: Shoot, lover.

My name. It's not Jack—it's Blake.

For real?

For real.

Damn, that's sexy. ;)

Your turn.

???

Tell ME something.

There's a long pause. He puts a hand to his face and seems to sense her there, who she says she is. Not fishy. Briny. The smell of the ocean. Salt water. Waves shedding spray in the wind. Then ten digits appear on the screen. Phone number, area code first.

The girl is healthy and beautiful. Her name is Beatrice, which Blake doesn't like; but Katie wanted a family name. They call her Bee. Truthfully, he doesn't like that either. To be honest, until recently, he hasn't liked the baby. It's nothing personal, or unexpected. There had been a year of debate leading up to the disposal of birth control. Blake wasn't ready for children; Katie was. Even after she went off the pill, they weren't really on the same page. They made love anyway. A lot. Katie was all over him, in a way she hadn't been since the beginning. Sometimes it was great. He felt like he was twenty again. His old confidence in the power of sex, his old certainty about the immortality of their passion, came back to him. Other times, Blake just felt used. The act left a bad feeling all over him, and he wondered if this was how it felt to be a woman in a chauvinist world. Once or twice, he even had performance problems. Well, he wasn't in the mood, all right? How many times had he had to accept that same apology from her? Anyway, what did he look like, a sperm bank? She told him he was being ridiculous. She cried because she wanted them to want this together. But none of it made any sense to him. Not only did he not want it, he didn't want it so badly he couldn't maintain a goddamn erection. In the end, he got the job done. She got exactly what she wanted when she wanted it; and no sooner was she pregnant than she seemed to start drifting away.

❧

He carries the number in his wallet. When he takes it out and looks at it, he thinks: what a weird world. This world where you can find or ruin your destiny with a careless left-side click. He remembers, very clearly, his first visit to the website's home page. Twenty or so photographs. Mostly women. A few wore clothes (a bikini top, a see-through frock), but most were nude. Some photos showed a complete body; others, nothing but an erogenous zone. Screen names appeared beneath each image. Blake couldn't believe what he was seeing. He'd thought the days of free love had ended forever. But this made a key party look as simpleminded as a kissing booth. Two million people. For dollars a month, you could join this global orgy, trading naked pictures with women from another hemisphere or arranging a meeting with a girl two blocks away. Searching by age or race or measurements. And the photos. To be frank, the close-ups of breasts and vaginas (to say nothing of the male organs) made him slightly queasy. But the wider views. They magnetized him in a way no erotic image ever had before. A few he couldn't stop looking at, but not because they excited him. Not exactly. Their power was more mysterious than that.

As for Lorelei's pictures, to call them mysterious is to sort of miss the point. What they are is odd. Maybe bizarre.

Since making contact with her, he has stopped browsing through the profiles. But he saw at least a hundred in those first two weeks—not one of them like hers. It kind of unnerved him at first, not the photo as much as her insistence on its factuality. He wondered sometimes if she was a little kooky, the kind of girl who reads bad fantasy novels and tacks posters of unicorns to her bedroom walls. But over time, he has come to understand that it's a kind of game. Like domination. She makes the rules and he obeys. Mainly, when they chat, he has learned to never mention legs or feet; and he's gotten comfortable enough with the whole thing to refer in his dirty-talk to what she has instead. Fins. Tail. Slick iridescent scales that cover her behind and, in front, grow right up to (but not over) a pink vulva and clitoris. Strange how the more he envisions this body, the more credible it seems.

One night, they're having dinner on the porch. Not Blake and Lorelei; Blake and Katie. He has not dialed the number yet. A warm night. Summer still weeks away, but he notices each day the coastal fog massing over the hills, growing like a fungus in the heat. He stares down at the table. Two plastic take-out containers filled with rolls of sushi. Tuna, salmon, soft-shell crab. It's ridiculous, but he can't do it. Katie's had two pieces, and she's dipping a third in soy sauce when she notices he's not eating.

It's getting cold, she says.

I thought I told you.

What?

I'm not eating sushi anymore.

She just narrows her eyes, speculative and concerned—the same look she gets when she thinks the baby may have a fever. Overfishing, he explains. Sierra Club alert. Whole species going extinct. When his wife tells him these particular fish are not coming back to life, he nods his head reasonably and says it's all right, he'll just eat the rice and seaweed.

Then it comes. The day he will label, in the weeks that follow, as the day he fucked up. He's in his office after a long afternoon of student conferences, and he's staring at the phone number, and he's staring at his phone. He knows he is the one dialing, but he doesn't feel in control of his body. He has the sense that somewhere someone's holding a voodoo doll of him out an upper-story window.

Hello?

Opening lines have been fighting it out in his head for days. He's come up with a dozen sexy ones he thought were pretty good. Now that he's hearing her voice—gentle, young (she sounds more sixteen than eighteen)—they all sound lecherous to him. He nearly hangs up. Feels suddenly middle-aged, not to mention foolish. He hasn't just been getting off with her; he's been confiding in her. Hang up now. Cancel your membership and throw away this piece of paper with these numbers on it, and you will still have done nothing really wrong. How did it come to this? He was just going to look from a distance. It was going to be like peering through a high-powered telescope into the unreachable corners of space. Even if somehow, through some suspension of physical laws, getting there became a possibility, he didn't believe he'd ever actually try to. Now he's almost there, and he's not sure he can turn back. It seems like another lifetime, a past life, the days when he and Katie were really in love. Just kids who couldn't imagine any undertaking more important or strenuous than writing a dissertation. She was beautiful and brilliant; and despite being under constant romantic siege, she'd always been faithful to him. Her certainty was contagious. She's the one, he had heard himself say over and over again. There's no one else. But years later, he finds himself staring more and more at a luminous screen, as a heartsick feeling spreads through his chest; and finally, one afternoon when the fog is rolling in off the ocean, he is speaking into his office phone, saying: Lorelei, hi. It's me. Blake.

She tells him guilt is a frame of mind. He's not a bad person, just a little bit lonely and a little bit lost. A regular guy. Unhappily married. A father who loves his baby but isn't ready for her. Okay—if they meet, if they schedule a secret rendezvous, he will be cheating on his wife. But what does that matter, really, in the larger scheme of things? What does it reveal about a man besides what he's got and what he wishes he had? She says she knows how he feels. Like he's drowning. She says she knows exactly how to save him.

They don't make a date, but they start making plans. How and where. On one hand, there is still an element of unreality, a sense that this is all an act of imagination; on the other, an understanding that he's performing consequential actions. If he keeps this up, his world is going to change.

One night, he has a dream—true to life, like all of his dreams. He has always been very literal in this way. No codes or encryptions. A dream about his baby will feature his baby, doing or not doing the things babies are supposed to do. A dream about sexual dysfunction will feature a woman, a bedroom, a soft penis. His mind doesn't seem to be equipped with the apparatus that turns the everyday into the impossible. In this latest one, he's at the computer chatting erotically with an old student who has somehow been transformed into a mermaid. Then Katie appears suddenly at his shoulder and discovers the secret. When he wakes, he can't remember his wife's reaction. What he remembers is the dream's emotional pitch, a paradoxical feeling that everything was finally going to be all right.

Blake wonders if this is what he wants. To be discovered. Not to do this thing and get away with it and keep it secret forever. But to do it and have it come out and let the shock wave hit his marriage. Sometimes when they fight—and it is always the same fight, the same dumb peevishness, the predictable resentments of people being pushed to their limits—he imagines ushering her into the study and showing her his member profile page and the inbox full of saved electronic love letters and the two photos (not the third one) of the girl who wrote them. He isn't sure what the point would be, strategically speaking. To bomb her back to the Stone Age? Or to scare her, just enough, and stop himself before he goes too far?

He decides he can't go through with it. He can't meet this girl even once. If he does, he'll never be able to talk to his daughter about ethics. It's bad enough that he's going to have to lie about drug use. If he does this, there will always be weakness in their communication—his advice and admonitions will fade in and out like a poor radio signal. Children intuit these things. It's no longer a question of what to do, but of how to do it. How to extricate himself. The first thing is to get away from the computer. He can't stop her from e-mailing him; and he checks his inbox compulsively, heart racing, for new messages. Then there are the midnight hours they spend chatting. By contrast, since this all started, four weeks ago now, he has spent little time alone with Katie. Hasn't given her a single orgasm. The drought has not bothered her much. Once or twice, she's joked about it; once or twice, come on to him in the fashion of someone giving her time to a worthy charity. The second thing: to do it with his wife.

Surprise, he says, handing her the brochure for a seaside lodge up the coast.

You're giving me a lodge?

This weekend.

What do you mean, this weekend?

We're going. Just you and me. Overnight. My mother'll babysit.

She gives him that I'm-worried-this-may-be-a-fever look and reminds him that their daughter has never yet slept an entire night without her. It takes him half the evening to convince her. By the time she consents, she's falling asleep sitting up. Blake kisses her good night. He watches her climb the stairs, notes the smile showing faintly through the fatigue. He stays up but does not turn on the computer. Doesn't go anywhere near it.

ɤ

They drive the coastal highway. Blake can tell Katie's mind is on the baby. His own mind he intends to keep on the woman beside him: his wife, love of his life, mother of his child. It is an unmysterious coincidence that, as they travel toward the black road-map dot that represents their destination, they get closer to another black dot, situated farther north. He could've made different reservations and charted a course south or east, *away* from the girl he's trying to get away from. But west is where the ocean is, and the coast is nicer up here. Infinite ocean, the green hills, his wife's pale skin. Blake reaches for her hand. This road, the sea, her touch have always affected him. But today the exhilaration is narcotically intense. He attributes the sensation to the distance he is putting between himself and the computer. No matter that in terms of mileage, in terms of physical space, he's closing the gap between himself and his lover. He could be on the other side of the world; and as long as he had Internet access, he'd be closer to her than he is right now. He's only been gone a few hours. But the plan is already working. He can already see the way out. She doesn't really exist in this world he's moving through now, world of grass and road and sky. For all he knows, she doesn't exist at all, the girl in those pictures. The more he thinks about it, the more convinced of this he becomes. The whole thing is too good to be true. A beautiful, eighteen-year-old self-proclaimed nymphomaniac with a mermaid complex. The whole goddamn website is probably a hoax.

Arriving at the lodge, he feels better than he has in months. Almost as if he's emerging from a long depression. His marriage seems half-full instead of half-empty. Blake understands that there's been a fog, a shadow obscuring his sight. He thinks: my beautiful brilliant wife! She hasn't been lost, just went missing for a while. In the car, there'd been talk, the pseudo philosophy, the intellectual junk food they'd consumed after midnight all through graduate school—and tonight, there will be the hot loud love that used to piss off the neighbors. This is clear as soon as they walk into the room. There's a jacuzzi, candy red and shaped like a heart. A mirror on the ceiling over the bed. Shag carpet growing like moss on one wall; the other three papered with a panoramic photograph of eastern mountains in autumn leaf. They used to joke about places like this. Katie walks through the door, claps a hand over her mouth. She's horrified. She's psyched. She drops her shoulder bag and dives down on the round mattress and gazes up into the reflection.

Oh, baby, she says.

It's all vintage.

Not the sheets, I hope.

He joins her on the velvety blanket, gives her a long kiss on the lips. Afterwards, she lifts her head to survey the room once more. Her tone is tongue-in-cheek, but she's not just joking when she says: You remembered.

Dinner. Midway through the meal, the sun sets; the moon rises in a spotless sky. On this veranda above the ocean, the website seems almost funny to him. Half a bottle of wine and he can see the whole thing from an academic distance. That's what he is, after all. An academic. So is Katie. Neither of them teaches modern culture—they both have their heads in the past. She'd probably find the whole thing as amusing as he does. Back in the room, naked in the jacuzzi, he considers telling her. Not everything. Just the basics. How he'd been stoned in the middle of the night and happened onto something bizarre. The lengths people go to, he'd say. The creative effort. Like this one girl. Took a picture of herself from the waist up and joined it to a picture of a fish tail. The stuff she wrote, you got the feeling she really believed it. Weird, huh? If he could say just this much, he'd feel lighter, like he'd confessed on some level. He says nothing. They kiss and touch in the pulsing water. His wife does not look the least bit old to him; but he's very cognizant, as he finds his way inside her, of how distant their youth is. Back in their twenties, they'd bought completely into the alarmism of the day. Fears of viral disease, the logic of self-preservation. The website isn't just funny—it's disturbing. The speed, the ease of it. The total lack of inhibition. Safety and caution are out of date. The world has gotten strange around them.

In the morning, just hugging her causes milk to flow. My breasts, she says, are about to freaking burst. She pumps. Even after this unburdening, her body is a vision, more astonishing than any photograph. They have to head home. Blake is the one who points this out. Katie doesn't want to leave. Let's take a walk, she says. Up the beach a ways. It's only eight; an hour's walk and we'll still be home by noon.

Yes, he feels great. With the cool sand under his feet and the waves breaking one after another and her hand clasping his. What's more, he's actually looking forward to seeing his daughter. He could stand another day or two of this, he could wait that much longer. But the point is, he feels something. He misses her! All these months, worried he'd never know even that much love. Blake expects that he's about to turn a corner. Just out of sight, but close, a mellow acceptance is waiting. Maybe even contentment.

The ocean to their left, to their right the cliff. Then, up ahead: a mass of rock blocking the way. The waves break against it, bursting white. A dead end. But up close he notices that, after each wave, as the water recedes, a thin strip of sand shows. Better to turn back, given the advancing hour and the signs at the lodge warning of sleeper waves and the danger of drowning. But you could do it, you could get past the obstacle—and on the other side, you'd find a sheltered cove, a magic place.

A little further, he says.

We can't get past.

There's a path. See? Now, after the wave.

I don't know, Blake.

Here. Take my hand.

His tone is one of entreaty. *I can't explain, just trust me.* And he really can't explain—not to his wife, not to himself—the intensity of this urge. They just have to do this. He meets her eyes. She doesn't want to, but she won't deny him. He holds her hand.

Is this risky behavior? For all they know, there's nothing on the other side—no cove, no magic. Maybe nothing but sheer cliff, or maybe the shore drops off suddenly. He's heard stories. Of people swept away. One person taken and the other helpless to do anything but watch.

The next wave forms, a dark wrinkle on the water. It swells, crests, and breaks.

And they run.

Spike of fear in the chest. The first real terror he's known. A parent's terror. In these moments, in this constricted space—the rock on her side, the resurgent water on his—a life flashes before his eyes. Not his; his daughter's. Something missing from the girl's story. Gone. Lost forever in the sea. Katie grips his hand, hard. As the next wave builds, still they are running, the wet sand seeming to clot around their feet while pelicans glide over the morning-blue ocean, which is coming at them very fast, with a speed gathered, a violence pent up over more time than they can really comprehend. The father doesn't mean to leave, doesn't want to in his heart. But it's as though everything has been arranged. There's no way to stop it now. He doesn't think these thoughts, so much as he hears them. Not as words, but as a song that flows from the wave. Let go her hand. Letting go is the hard part. The rest is so easy.

THE CLIFFS AT MARPI

The only possible decision. If the worst comes to pass—if the Americans land, as they have already at Tarawa and Kwajalein, and are not stopped at the island's shores but push the army back to the central spine of mountains—Kimiko will take the children and walk north through Talafofo and Banadero to Marpi Point.

She has never been to the cliffs (which stand far to the north, a long way from the cane fields and the mill), but she still remembers her one sight of them, gained from the deck of the ship that carried her here. Five years ago now. Winter 1939. The vessel, called the *Saipan Maru*, had transported nearly one hundred people like herself, her husband, and their very young son across a thousand miles of ocean, southward, to this strange and wonderful colony. The morning of their arrival had been bright, dazzling. Kimiko stood on deck as they coasted through the lagoon, over water of otherworldly color; and she saw, off to the north, a wall of rock, dark as a storm cloud, very dark.

Okinawa, too, had its rocky heights. But she had never really seen those, not like this: from an offshore distance that made the giant mass unreal and small. She had never seen anything (she realizes now, looking back) in quite this way. For the first time in her life, *she* was the large thing, the great thing.

ℓ

They have been walking for a day now. The going is slow because the children are young and getting increasingly hungry. And the summer heat is tremendous. They have seen older people on the road, infirm people losing their balance, overwhelmed by the sun. They have also seen dead bodies. Some give an impression of peaceful sleep; others seem to have been torn apart, picked apart by wild animals.

Her oldest is six.

The boy stares at these figures. Stops and stares. She has to pull him away.

ℓ

The decision was mutual, made by them both. By Ryuji and Kimiko. Husband and wife, father and mother. Parents of three children. A son, six; a daughter, four; and the baby, not yet one. She knows she agreed to this. She has known for some time (since her husband's conscription six months ago) that, if the time came to go to Marpi, she would have to take the children there by herself. However, now that they're on their way, the idea seems to have no natural relation to her. On the road, there are moments when she can't remember where the idea came from and when she even forgets what it is. They are walking to nowhere in particular, merely walking. Then the thunderclap of an exploding artillery shell will shock her back into full awareness; her breath will stop in her throat, as if hands are seizing her there, wrapping a rope of hemp around her neck and pulling hard. Suddenly, she's the one standing still, and it's one of the children who takes her hand and tugs.

To them, the cliffs mean refuge. This is not a misconception. She has not lied to her children. She has told them they will all be safer in Marpi. Beyond the reach of the Americans. This is the truth.

The invaders have been here for a week now. They were not stopped on the beaches. They've pushed the defense forces back to the mountains. Now Kimiko and many others are crossing these mountains, moving north. Not only company people like herself, not only Okinawans. But Japanese, Chamorros, Kanakas. It's strange how in the jungle, on the road to Marpi, they all seem the same somehow. Difficult to tell apart. As if, in fear, they've all shed an outer skin and lost the characteristics that made them who they were, made some superior to others.

Certainly to the Americans, they are all equal. Kimiko knows the enemy will see no distinctions, make no exceptions. They will rape and torture regardless of race, social standing, age. Stories of their cruelty have been circulating for years, ever since the war began; but in the past few months, the stories have proliferated and grown terrifyingly dark. The Americans have brought terror across the ocean, possessing one island after another like some ancient evil spirit. For a long time, she didn't believe they could make it this far, this close to her home. No one did. But now they're here, on the other side of this very mountain! And that, she reminds herself, is why she is taking her children to Marpi. Kimiko has never laid eyes on an American. She must see to it that none of them ever does.

ₐ

They spend the first night in a cave, the jungle outside lighting up with flashes of man-made light. There are others with them, how many she's not sure; and she's not sure who they are. No one speaks. She can't see her own hand in front of her face. Tomorrow, it should be possible to reach the railway tracks that snake around the island's northern perimeter and can be followed all the way to the cliffs. The trains stopped moving sugar weeks ago. Nearly all the cane fields have been burned, set afire from the air. The mill has been destroyed in the same manner. But if the northern tracks are still passable, maybe a train will come to carry them on flatcars the rest of the distance. If not, she's not sure how she will make it so far with a baby in her arms, this infant whom she has hardly let go of since morning. He is not a weightless child. He has his father's build. The muscles in her arms feel frayed. She could probably lay him down now on the dirt floor without waking him. But she doesn't. Only once today did she set him down (to wipe him clean with some leaves); and this simple separation caused her to reel with dizziness, with a violent sensation of falling, spinning through space—as if without him as ballast, she couldn't keep her world steady.

꙳

Kimiko and Ryuji are both Okinawans. They have understood since childhood that they are second-class citizens, not true Japanese. Backward, lazy, poor. From farms whose crops never seemed to come to anything. Growing up, they dreamed of Nan'yō. Green islands with names like Ponape, Kusiae, Saipan. In Kimiko's imagination, the islands were paradise, jewels strung across the ocean. To Ryuji, they were this and more. It was his idea, after they married, to apply for work with Nan'yō Kōhatsu. They presented their paperwork (copies of the family registers, certificates of good health) and were offered third-class passage on a cargo liner, six hectares of land, money for agricultural tools, living expenses for the first year of their contract. It was all too good to be true!

Weeks later, they boarded a spectacular vessel, newly built and weighing over four thousand tons—a floating city with luxurious staterooms, a cocktail bar, library, movie theater. Their own accommodations, of course, were small and austere (tatami matting, an oilskin-covered table), and they weren't allowed in the theater. But for both of them it was enough to be near these things, to be part of the world they existed in. At night in the dark, as the ship steamed effortlessly through the sea, Kimiko's mind would fill with visions of everything happening on the decks above her, and her heart overflowed with strange emotions. She wasn't just a villager anymore. She was a colonist, an adventurer, a seed carrying over the ocean.

It wouldn't be easy, this new life. The company's recruitment officers had made that very clear. Long months of labor in the fields, in a climate that could wither the spirit, in isolation that could unhinge the mind. But she felt a desire, almost romantic, for the coming labors and hardships, which she imagined would be like the hardships of childbirth, pains that would give way to an indescribable happiness.

Nan'yō!

In the dark on the tatami mat, she would hear the noise of a party coming from another third-class cabin. Someone plucking the cheap strings of a sanshin, drunken people singing some foolish love song. No wonder they were looked down on. Kimiko and Ryuji agreed—they wanted nothing to do with this old way of life. In Nan'yō they were going to become Japanese. And years from now when they returned home on this ship, they would move freely through the higher decks, sleeping in a stateroom paneled with dark wood, basking in the moonlike glow of a samurai film. That is, if they cared to return home at all.

⟨

Before sunrise, they are walking again. The baby in her arms; one child at her left, the other at her right. The younger, the girl, can't keep up. She cries. Asks, again and again, to be carried like the baby.

By noon they still haven't reached the tracks. They've eaten nothing since yesterday afternoon. The fighting, which they've been hearing all morning to the south, is getting fiercer, louder, closer. It's not just the sound of small arms fire and rockets, but the awful blasts from the naval vessels offshore. The shelling is coming from the east now, which means the bombs are passing overhead, moving faster than anything she has ever seen, their iron bodies flashing with sun before they collide with the mountain, the highest point on the island, throwing up storms of rock and smoke.

Meanwhile, Kimiko stands quarreling in the road with her children. Her daughter won't budge from a sitting position in the dirt. Her son wants to find his father. Find him. As if he's hiding from the boy, the way he would sometimes hide in the cane, calling out: Kenji!

She hasn't seen Ryuji for two weeks.

His regiment had been assigned to the airfield in the south, which by now has almost certainly been lost.

❧

An hour later, at a junction (where another road runs west, to the shore where the invasion began), they meet a family with an oxcart. Chamorros. On their way to a farm in Talafofo. The man leads the animal; a woman and a child ride in the cart; and another child—unborn, probably eight months along—rides inside the woman.

There isn't any space, but they make some. They share fruit, taro, coconut milk. Like many of the tōmin, they speak Japanese. Better than Kimiko. They grew up with the language; they're fluent. There's something unfair, very wrong, about this. They ask her where she is going.

Marpi.

The answer seems to worry them. From the moment she saw them, they have looked scared; now they look scared for her. The man shakes his head. The pregnant woman says, No, you stay at the farm, there's an underground shelter already dug. Kimiko says nothing. Then, finding her manners, bows her head. Despite her anger, she bows; and she reminds herself that these people are savages, good but ignorant. They don't understand. As she falls asleep sitting up, baby at her breast, she thinks: These foolish tōmin! Don't they care what will happen to them, don't they care about their children? Kimiko noticed, as soon as she climbed into the cart, a small statue of a Christian goddess. Blue robe, hands folded together, band of light encircling her head. All their churches destroyed (as her own shrines have been destroyed), yet they go on believing their gods will somehow protect them. And they look at her as though she's the one with strange and disturbing ideas.

꒚

When she wakes up, flat out on the ground, she thinks she's in the cane field. She must've fainted in the heat. She actually smiles, thinking of what her husband will say when she tells him she fainted. Nan'yo is no place for idlers and weaklings. It only lasts an instant, this floating in time. Then she remembers the baby. He was in her arms, is no longer. Standing up abruptly causes the road to pitch and she falls back down. Only now can Kimiko really see what's in front of her. The bloody remains of the ox; a wheel of the cart, burning; her oldest sitting in the road with blood-wet hair, blinking his eyes. She stands again, more carefully this time. Looks behind her. In a tangle of ferns and vines, she sees the other two. The girl cradling the baby, the baby crying. She can barely hear him. His voice is the small, high whine of a mosquito. As for the continuing explosions, they might be nothing but distant waves crashing on sand. Her ears are numb, the world is nearly silent. Recalling a silent film they once saw in town—crying suddenly at the thought that she will never watch another moving picture, never feel the trade winds again, never see the flame trees bloom in spring—she walks unsteadily forward. Takes the baby in her arms. Takes her daughter's hand, and leads her out to where her brother is still sitting, staring as if in a trance. When Kimiko reaches him, she finally sees what he sees, which has been hidden from her by the wreckage of the cart and the body of the ox. The pregnant woman lying motionless in the dirt, her belly torn open; and one arm of the baby reaching out, grasping at thin air. There are two men, two white-skinned soldiers, kneeling there with her. Americans. Kimiko doesn't move. Her feet are like roots. The soldiers don't appear to have guns or swords. And they don't seem to see her. One is motioning down the road, south; the other is shaking his head and holding his hand out, demanding something. Suddenly, she comes to her senses. Her boy won't stand up, or can't. So she grips his wrist and drags him across the road. She never takes her eyes off the men. What she sees is this: one handing the other a knife, the knife cutting into the woman's stomach. They cut into her like she's some kind of animal. Kimiko can hardly breathe now. The road is tilting again as she muscles her children into the jungle. Leaf by leaf, the foliage obscures her view; but before the road slips from sight, she glimpses the tiny infant being raised up from its mother, the umbilical cord uncoiling, the bloody knife.

❧

She shouldn't return to the road, but there's nothing else to do. The jungle is impassable. They fight their way through the vines and underbrush for a hundred meters, then find their way back.

To the south, she expects to see tanks, men in green uniforms. Nothing yet. Maybe another hour of daylight. Perhaps the enemy won't come much farther today. But they'll have to hurry.

She runs.

This is how she gets the children moving. By scaring them into thinking she'll leave them behind. Already, she's unsure of what she just witnessed. She doesn't know what the Americans were doing with that knife. Can't say why, for what purpose, they were removing the baby.

{ }

By nightfall, they have reached another junction, turned east toward the sound of waves, and discovered an isolated cove, sandy, walled by volcanic rock. The ocean is violent here, not safe for bathing, but she manages to wash the dirt and blood off everyone. Her oldest is the only one with a real injury. A gash on the crown of his head, which bleeds a lot but appears to be superficial. Impossibly, they're all whole. Kimiko can't decide how she feels about this. Part of her wants to give thanks to every spirit she can think of; another part wonders if being spared is actually a form of punishment.

The children lie down on the sand. Kimiko can't sleep. She watches the sky, and as it turns dark yet quick with stars, the confusion in her mind only deepens. She must admit: a confusion has been there all along, ever since she and her husband first discussed what to do if things got very bad.

He had his uniform by then, his long sword and pistol. It was a winter evening—the trade winds blowing, the air almost cool—when he told her what the men in his regiment were saying. The defeat at Kwajalein had been more severe than anyone knew. Same with Truk. Soon, Ryuji said, the devil will be here. And we won't be able to stop him either. We won't win. She thought then about the convoys that had been leaving for weeks already, taking colonists home. One of them had been torpedoed before it even got out of the archipelago. But even if they were willing to take such a risk, they could never get on one of those ships. Not enough money; and the company had only given them one-way tickets.

Kenji had come out of the house then, wanting to know what they were talking about. Nothing, Kenji-chan. They sent the boy back in, but a trace of him seemed to remain; and the rest of their conversation was as awkward and indirect as if they were trying to discuss, in front of the child, some matter unfit for his ears. Her husband talked about being strong. The importance of not succumbing, not surrendering. Don't forget, Kimiko. How far from home we came, how hard we worked to change and improve ourselves. We can't let all that effort come to nothing. We can't let it end in dishonor. The sugarcane moved in the wind. The whole field trembling and trying to hush him, and she too trembling, like a cherry blossom losing its hold on leaf and bark, soon to fall fluttering to the ground.

ح

And all night she can't stop thinking of the woman. She drops off into sleep, but keeps seeing her body in the road and the baby's hand reaching out of it. She isn't sure if she's dreaming or thinking when she sees herself in the road, dead, and her own baby in white hands.

Then her eyes are open.

The ocean breathing heavy. The stars still shining over her.

ح

Finally, the tracks. A single set, narrow gauge, built to transport harvested cane to the refineries in the south. Here at the railway's northern end, there's a kind of station house, deserted now; a toylike steam engine; and a lot of empty flatcars, which seem to be waiting for the farmers to come with their crop. Kimiko has never been so far north. But she's heard about this land, which is flat and plentiful, far from town but near to the railway.

She thought that every green thing had been burned up in the aerial bombings. Everything lost forever. But there's color here!

Along the tracks, flowers bloom. Butterflies wheel through the air. Birds call and dart from the brush. As they walk, they can see emerald cane fields and savannahs of sword grass stretching off to blue water. They break off stalks of cane and suck the juice. The fighting is off to the west, on the other side of the ridge, which seems tall and mighty enough to keep the war away from here forever. She knows it won't. Their world is curling up and blackening like paper in a fire. The flames just haven't reached this place yet.

But she can't understand how it's come to this. She remembers, so clearly, the day she started believing in victory. Two years ago now. A brilliant winter day. An automobile driving down the town's main street of crushed coral; a voice, amplified by a loudspeaker, announcing the incredible news. *The American fleet destroyed!* All at once, that bright white way was full of people—shopkeepers, postmen and policemen, housewives with parasols, maids, schoolchildren, government officials in smart white uniforms, cane farmers—shouting and cheering. A celebration two days long. Fireworks painting the night sky. Sake for everyone. Sweet wine to make your head spin and give you the eyes of a diviner. How bright the future was going to be. What a happy destiny, it seemed, to be living here and now—at this momentous time, under this everlasting flag.

To be Japanese in Nan'yō.

≀

And to be American. What does that mean? To drop bombs day and night, set whole worlds on fire, sink passenger ships at sea, capture women and children and cut them to pieces, cut babies out of their dead mothers. Why? Cut them out and then what? Then what?

᪥

They're close now. Tomorrow, after one more night, they'll be at the cliffs—and on this last night, while the sky above the ridge pulses with yellow-orange light, her dreams are of falling. She wakes with a start, her body hitting the ground as if she'd been levitating in her sleep, the impact forcing the breath from her lungs. Her first impulse is to check on the children, as if they've fallen with her and might be injured, or worse. This happens three times. Each time, she finds her daughter and baby asleep, her older son awake, watching her in the light from the distant fires.

In the past few days, Kenji has changed somehow. Maybe it's just a mother's imagination—but with every mile walked, his face seems to gain complexity, like a face being carved from wood. The closer they get to Marpi, the more suspicious he seems of why they're going there. At certain moments—like now, deep in this field of sword grass, in this ghostly glow—he seems to be asking of Kimiko a wordless question, one he doesn't fully understand and doesn't want the answer to. In a whisper, she tells him to sleep. No sooner does he obediently shut his eyes than she regrets giving the instruction. All of a sudden, her heart is beating very urgently. There's a day she's thinking of, so long ago now. Before Nan'yō. Kenji's first birthday, when they offered him on a tray (according to a silly outmoded ritual) four objects. An abacus counter, a coin, a plate of food, and a pencil. Nobody took the ceremony or its portents very seriously, but the whole family groaned when her son chose the pencil. Oh, a poet! Better have another son quick, Kimiko. Better have two to make up for this daydreamer.

The next day, they discover a piece of paper on the tracks. Kenji sees it first, picks it up, and reads silently. He's only six, but he understands Japanese as well as any of them and speaks it without a trace of rustic accent.

Lifesaving leaflet.

Kimiko can see these characters, the largest and boldest ones, from a few feet away; but for a few moments, she has no idea what they could possibly mean. When she tries to take the object into her own hands, the boy says *he* found it. He walks away from her, staring at this thing. She's not sure why (it hardly seems reasonable under the circumstances), but his defiance makes her angry.

Kenji, give me that.

No. It's mine.

Kenji.

No.

She almost voices an old threat. When your father hears about this. When he gets back from the field, back from town, the railway, the mill. But, of course, there's no field anymore, no mill, no town. She has known, for some time now, that all these things are gone. Still, she feels a shock, not unlike the one she felt the other day when she woke up and found the oxcart burning and couldn't keep her balance, couldn't hear, couldn't believe what she was seeing.

Next thing she knows, the leaflet is in her hands and her son is down on the tracks. She has never struck him before. Her hand stings from the contact, and her eyes burn as they range over the writing. *Come slowly toward the American line. Good treatment will be accorded. Do not approach American lines at night. Food, clothing, medical treatment. Come one by one. Come slowly with hands raised high above your head and carry only this leaflet.* There's a long moment before she starts tearing it to pieces, a long look south, back the way they came—and a picture in her mind, unreal as a dream, of everything returning to normal, all of them together again, starting over.

ʔ

She is not thinking clearly. She shouldn't have torn up the leaflet. Never should've hit her son. It's noon, not long after the making of these mistakes, when they hear the train. Heavy mechanical breathing. Dark smoke over the palm trees, then the little black locomotive. The flatcars are loaded with people. Civilians and soldiers. Almost all of them Japanese, Okinawan. Climbing onto the end car, Kimiko can't stop herself from hopefully scanning the faces of the soldiers.

The train is not moving fast. Why then does it seem to her to be out of control? Not crawling on a flat plain, but hurtling down some impossible gradient.

Suddenly, she is thinking of a song that, for a time last year, she hadn't been able to get out of her head. She would hear it on the radio in the company store or floating through the windows of the company club, where some clerk or manager was always playing it on a phonograph. *We are ready, just like blooming flowers that will fall / Let's fall beautifully for our country.*

ʔ

The song. The leaflet. A mother in the road and a tiny fist reaching out of her. Even if they were helping, even if they were saving its life, then what? Now nurse it, raise its parents from the dead, bring the fields back to life.

ʔ

There is more than one place to jump from. The cliff at the island's northern point, which drops straight into the ocean; and the one farther inland, the end of the mountain spine, which is infinitely higher and drops off not onto water but onto rock. The train is going to the point. It's almost there when the other cliff comes into view. Some people on the train gesture wildly, others look away. To Kimiko, who just stares, the distant falling people really do look like flower blossoms. The way their kimonos unfold in the wind. As the train comes to a stop (just short of the airfield, where the tracks have been mangled by bombing), a soldier climbs on top of the locomotive and starts giving instructions. Kimiko doesn't seem to hear him; but as she gets down from the flatcar, his words are echoing in her ears. *Better to be a crushed jewel.* His is not the only voice. Another, amplified by a loudspeaker, is saying something different. *Do not throw away your invaluable life for such a lie.* This other voice. Japanese, but not truly. The pronunciation is poor, the accent foreign. Inferior to her own, as her own has always been inferior.

⟨

There's nothing real about the voice, just as there's nothing real about this place, these last few square meters before deadly air into which families are jumping; also huddling together and pulling the pins of grenades, but mostly pushing one another off the cliff. Not real. Not the end of a war, not the end of the world. More like the far end of a dream. In the dream, Kimiko stands on the landing strip. Baby in her arms; daughter hugging one leg; first-born son holding her hand and then, without warning, releasing it. He doesn't even look up, doesn't look at her before he starts running. Her impulse, naturally, is to run after him, to call for him, though she realizes as she lets him go toward that foreign voice and its promises of humane treatment that the only reason she wants to stop him is to say good-bye. What's wrong with her? What kind of mother is she? Insofar as she is asking herself anything, she is asking herself these questions as she finds the superhuman strength to lift her daughter into one arm while shifting the baby into the other. She carries the children closer to the edge. Down below, bodies are being rocked by the waves, carried slowly into deeper water. Also getting caught up in conflicting white surges and going nowhere. A cloud moves over the sun. The wind, a faint one coming off the ocean, seems cold against her wet skin. If they survive the fall and continue to feel, the water, too, will be very cold. Nearby, a family is forming an orderly line. The youngest child in the front, closest to the edge. It happens fast. One after another they disappear.

ξ

Kimiko stares at the empty space they leave behind. For a few moments, there are no gunshots, no grenades exploding, no one screaming. Only that enemy voice, echoing off the rocks of the point, coming from everywhere and nowhere.

Making promises.

She doesn't know what to believe anymore. But she let Kenji go. Let him go as if she loved him differently, less or more than these two still in her arms. Suddenly, tears are streaming down her face. How foolish it all was, from the very start! To think this place could belong to them. As she tries to get her breath, she can't help feeling that she always knew better. Nothing could stay so green. Now she, too, promises something. To hold both of them all the way down. She says this to her daughter. I'll hold both of you, I won't let you go. But once they start falling, she can't keep her grip. The girl is torn away as the ocean overturns and night seems all at once to fall in the middle of day, all the stars falling with them, and finally the only thing left to the mother is the baby.

frannycam.net/diary

nearly xmas eve. merry merry. this will be my final
entry. thanks everyone for the emails the ecards
the wishes the love the friendship :) you've seen me
thru so much these last weeks and i hope i can rely
on you all for one final gift. forgiveness. i solemnly
swear that what i am about to do (what you are
watching) is real. that's what this is all about, right?
reality? i'd never play tricks on you all. i love you too
much.

so how can i do this in front of you? the thing
is how can i not? how could i deny you the most
private moment? snowing now. why is it that the
world seems deaf on a snowy night? sorry about the
tears. sorry about the suspense. sorry sorry sorry.
see you in the archives.

love always, francesca

DECEMBER 21 AT 7:42 P.M.

saw Z today. told her if anything ever happens to me, i want her to have the whole kit n kaboodle—and then i started explaining how i want to be cremated. "no perverted morticians feeling up my dead body, ok Z?" she went pale as a zombie.

"F," she said, "is this a 911 call?"

"no, Z," i said. "its my last will and testament. one of these days, i'm going to shoot myself online. i want you to know what to do afterwards."

slowly the color drained back into her face. "god, F," she said, "for a second there, i thought you were serious."

i pressed my face back into the warmth of her. skin with hot blood flowing inside it. rivers and streams and tributaries of blood. she pulled the blanket tighter around us and kissed me.

does that turn you on?

DECEMBER 19 AT 11:57 P.M.

maybe you all were right. maybe i shouldnt have gone. sister flora stopped by today but i didnt want to see her. i dont want to see anyone. i dont want to see anything. there are certain things, once you've watched them, there's nothing left worth looking at.

there's another one tonite. i could hear dad crying in the shower before. nearly midnight now. hour when souls are torn from bodies. what a

neighborhood. what a job. question for the magic 8
ball: is my true love in the bardo realm experiencing
the radiance of the clear light of pure reality?
answer: try again later.

just got back from group. today we heard from lydia
whose best friend died of a fatal sex disease. last
week it was theo who lost his brother in a head-on
vehicular cataclysm with an eighteen-wheeler. we.
we ten. we in all our we-ness. we are a flock of lost
sheep. other forces that have punched holes in our
hearts include drug overdose, murder, malignant
neoplasm, and suicide. and then of course there's
me. next week is my turn to share. butterflies
already aflutter. group has a strange effect on you.
it calms you like a drug. then wears off like a drug.
seems like the same things happen to all of us, and
our minds and bodies all have the same reactions.
most people think that's comforting. me? it just
makes me more afraid.

yours, franny

p.s. sorry about yesterday's entry. i know you know
i didnt mean it. i'm not myself these days.

symbols letters images! all meaningless! see this?
(!) it's an exclamation point. it means i'm shouting.
see this? :(it's a sad face. sadness is made of a colon
and a parenthesis. see this? this is a streaming video
image of the face of someone who is nothing but a

colon and a parenthesis. nothing but a symbol. what
are you looking at anyway? why don't you all go
blind yourselves! go stare at a f***ing eclipse! JUST
LEAVE ME ALONE!

DECEMBER 11 AT 2:01 P.M.

surprised to see me this afternoon? one of those
days. we all have them, right? bad hair. mutinous
tampons. psychotic episodes in science lab. they
sent me home on indefinite rest leave pending
psychiatric evaluation. i'm not getting out of this
unstigmatized. so i'm crazy and mrs flanzbaum is
just doing her job.

can anyone give me a good reason why a seventh
grader in this day and age needs to see the insides
of an executed amphibian?

make incision. pin back skin. observe internal
organs, musculature, bloodless veins. look.
peer at everything inside. savor sweet smell of
formaldehyde. roughly two minutes into operation,
inform teacher you are finished. when she says you
cant possibly be finished, toss severed head of frog
onto desk and commence shrieking. go hysterically
unto the principal's office.

DECEMBER 9 AT 11:32 A.M.

a field of white wooden crosses at the end of a long
dirt road. between the snow on the ground and the
sun glare, the markers were practically invisible.
i waited for my eyes to adjust but the light only
got brighter the closer we came to putting him

in the ground. the bare trees nothing but pencil sketches while inkblot people lifted an inkblot box and made it disappear. not into a hole. into a black parallelogram cut neatly into the mirror of snow.

the memorial service? not an empty seat in the house. he left a lot of friends behind. mostly men, of course. and me. it was a nondenominational affair. no hymns. but the choir made sounds like angels and the jazz band played "take the a train." no prayers either. but we had poetry and reminiscences and his favorite joke about the two geckos who walk into a bar and instructions from the tibetan book of the dead. hard not to cry. hard not to laugh too, and hard not to tap your feet to the music. at the end, as they carried the coffin out, someone stood up and started to applaud. then someone else and someone else. until pretty soon we were all on our feet, clapping and whistling. like he'd given some great performance and if we cheered long and hard enough, he'd come back to do an encore.

DECEMBER 7 AT 11:11 P.M.

sent Z another apology email today (subject: PLEASE DON'T IGNORE THIS followed fifteen minutes later by a second (DID YOU READ IT?) then a third (I KNOW YOU'RE ONLINE) and a fourth (I'M GOING TO CALL YOU). thirty seconds later i was hearing her voice for the first time in a week. "castaneda residence," she said. "oh, Z," i said.

there was a long silence. I was sitting on the bed, a few feet from the cam. "i know you're watching

me," i said. "i can't sleep. i talk to you but you don't
hear me." i moved closer to the laptop, stared
into the little camera eye. "reply," i said, "please."
i listened to her breathe. taking air into her lungs
and letting it out. deep doctor's-office breaths, and
i thought of moving a stethoscope all around her
body, listening to her insides making sounds of
life. then a new message! subject: I FORGIVE YOUR
DUMB ASS. i sighed out loud, like a character in a
comic strip. "F," she said. "yes, Z?" "there's just one
thing." "whats that?" "you've got a snot in your left
nostril."

DECEMBER 3 AT 9:39 A.M.

hitting the road for a few days. my parents say i
need help :(web access will be limited but i'll try
somehow to log on and visit the chat room.

per my absence, i have added a few days to your
time if you are already a frannycam family member.
out of sight out of mind? i hope not.

hugs, franny

DECEMBER 2 AT 12:01 P.M.

36 hours later. snowing. five inches so far. maybe
it'll stay for xmas. i have a very modest list this year.
in fact, i only want one thing. so you can forget
about the clothing, gift certificates, jewelry, ebooks,
ipods, mp3s, and calico kittens. you can forget
about standing in long lines, parting with hard
earned cash, and saving receipts. you can forget the
gift wrap, the ribbons, and the bows, secrecy and

surprises, chestnuts roasting, silver bells, and red-nosed reindeer. i don't want any of that.

i just want him back.

i want him to live again. to breathe, see, hear, smell, taste . . . love me. all i want is a quiet little miracle.

DECEMBER 1 AT 4:03 P.M.

four p.m. just woke up. cant understand last nite's entry. must have written it just after. when i got home. but i dont remember writing it. i dont remember coming home.

i remember the curtain closing. i remember people with candles. dozens of candles. a galaxy of tiny stars. and i remember watching. watching every moment, not looking away, not even blinking. thinking . . . this is death. so ordinary, so real, you just want more.

DECEMBER 1 AT 1:19 A.M.

the strangest dream. waking up feels like being born again, like being set free. haven't felt like this since that nite last spring. have i ever told you about it? me and Z and a hundred others all high as kites. the place was like the inside of some giant heart pumping color and beating so loud you couldnt hear anything else. i didnt know where my body ended and the air began. house of spirit-love. place of lucid dreaming. can you see the clear light? that is the infallible mind of dharma kaya. if you can recognize it, the wheel of

rebirth will be stopped and you will find freedom
aka nirvana. if not, you will move thru the bardo
realm and be blown by the winds of karma into a
new womb. don't be afraid, o nobly-born so-and-
so's! we only fear death because we dont remember
what its like. we cant remember the last time we
died or the time before or the time before that.
if we could, we'd realize that these bodies of ours
are nothing. nothing but meat. and we'd welcome
another chance to embrace the pure light, to stop
our wandering. to exist in a place without flesh. to
interface with the all-good, the divine mind, the
clear light of pure reality. Z, you chameleon, you
color changer. dance with me! we can make the
whole world spin faster under our feet. F, she said,
i adore you. and then she kissed me and all the
boundaries were suddenly gone. this happiness . . .
will it never end?

i love you all, franny

NOVEMBER 30 AT 10:01 P.M.

two hours left. no, i'm not sure if this is the right
thing to do. but it doesn't help any, all of you trying
to talk me out of it. sometimes we make mistakes
in life with our eyes wide open. does that make
us heroes or cowards? my father talked to me this
afternoon. he warned me. said the worst part is the
peacefulness of it. i said something terrible to him
then, something i can't bear to repeat. then i shied
away from his hand. i might as well have knifed him
in the heart.

so i go over to Z's after school today. she wants to sit around and read her new mags. fine. latest issues of "bitch rag" "angry young woman" and "twat!" there we are digesting all sorts of edifying journalism about menstrual anarchy, bruised hymens, and other grrrl-related marginalia, when i realize i need her now. more than i ever have.

i tell her everything. every crazy thing. the weird wonderful things that have already happened. the impossible horrible things that will happen soon. and while i'm at it, while secrets are rushing out of me in a flood, i sit down at her laptop. i type the address of my site. my other name. my other life. the image of my bedroom appears on the screen. with no expression on her face, she reaches for the touch pad. clicks on the archives. and there i am. close and faraway. sitting down and standing up. clothed and unclothed.

she looks at me like she's about to either burst into tears or beat me senseless with a combat boot. i watch from her window while she marches out back with a baseball bat to the rusting hulk of the old cadillac. it's been there forever, that car, ever since she was a little girl. in the spring, when the rain comes, it sinks a little deeper into the earth. in the winter the wheel rims freeze into the mud. someday centuries from now, i guess what's left of it will be totally buried, a fossil waiting for someone to come along and dig it up and put its bones back together.

Z enjoys speeding this process along. two side windows are gone, a taillight, both headlights. there goes the windshield.

with the louisville slugger still in hand, she assesses the damage. then she looks up at me. "go home," she says. "and dont come back."

NOVEMBER 27 AT 8:44 P.M.

hunger strike, day two. although my father is worried, he seems to respect this strategy of mine. my mother, on the other hand, has washed her hands of the entire affair. if you die of starvation, you'll have no one but yourself to blame. such is the look she gives me after she says grace and i start watching my dinner cool. my mother, the stormy-weather catholic. does she even know that all thru history there have been girls blessed with a special kind of love, who could live for months, even years without eating a bread crumb? people would come from miles around to look at them. just to see them. and then of course there are the saints of ronald reagan middle school, grade 7. saint chloe and saint amber and saint sabrina . . . but i am not one of them. i can't stand the feeling of a finger down my throat.

when he came up to my room tonite, with that bowl of chicken soup, i knew i'd outlasted them. but i didnt feel victorious or superior. i just felt old. like an old woman trapped in a young girl's body. still, i let him crumble saltines into the broth, the way he used to. i let him spoon-feed me, as if i were still

his innocent daughter. and i thought of all your
eyes watching him and him not knowing you were
there. "dont do it," i finally said. "if you dont do it,
i dont have to see it." and all of a sudden i sensed
how much weight was pressing down on his heart.
the child in me wanted to fold her arms around
him. the woman said no. don't ever get close to him
again.

NOVEMBER 25 AT 1:01 P.M.

my mother took me to church this morning so i
could be properly put to shame. the idea being that
statues of virgins, stained glass doves, and prayers
about the sins of the world would inspire me to
fits of weeping, pleas for forgiveness, and other
miscellaneous groveling. didnt work. not only did i
not shed a single tear, i refused to take communion.
i just sat in the pew like a political protestor. my
mother: furious. the car ride home: wordless.
outside: bare trees, a cold rain drizzling, trailer
homes with satellite dishes in the yards pointed
hopefully toward space, bullet-holed signs warning
motorists about hitchhikers.

the house was empty. my father, i knew, had gone
to work. he's a secular humanist. weeks like this, we
never see much of him anyway. there's so much to
do, so much to hide from us. i was halfway up the
stairs when she finally spoke to me. she said, "you're
not going." like its a date, a dance, a party. as if
being there wont be the worst kind of punishment.
"all right," i said. "then i'm not eating."

where to begin? i can hardly type. no sleep and my
poor eyes. i dont think i'll ever cry again. but so
many questions re: last nite. are you all concerned
or just curious? do you care or do you just want to
be turned on by the smutty details? i'm not sure i
care anymore.

yes that was my psycho mother. and yes that was
blood she was looking for and blood she found. yes
HE was the one. yes it felt good and yes it hurt. yes
i am grounded for life. yes it happened there and no
i cant tell you how i got inside. yes it was his first
time too. yes i am in love with him. yes i said yes
and no i did not say no. no it was not safe and yes i
know it was foolish. yes mother, yes yes yes, i am a
ruined flower. i am your priceless china in pieces on
the floor. yes i am frightened.

NOVEMBER 23 AT 8:09 P.M.

woke up today feeling strangely optimistic. like
maybe everything's going to turn out all right in
the end. then i find a ray of hope in my inbox! the
power of positive thinking :) follow the link below
and add your name to the petition, then forward it
to as many friends as possible. its not too late!

http://www.savesasha.com

re: last night's entry. i dont mean to accuse you all.
i know there are a lot of people in this family who
care. so here's your chance to step up and put your
feelings into action.

xoxo, franny

btw—secret rendezvous scheduled. i'll see him,
touch him, hold him soon.

NOVEMBER 22 AT 6:44 P.M.

the vultures started circling today. they hear that
death is in the area and in come the vans, the
transmitters, the video cameras. same old story.
but this time they're early and there are so many
of them. more than i've ever seen before. their idea
of breaking news: that time is passing, that time
is running out. the sun rises and sets and they are
here to tell us about it. inside (their sources say)
preparations are under way, the mood is tense.
meanwhile, there are nationwide polls to be taken.
politicians to be interviewed. experts to be quizzed
on the legal and ethical blah blah blah of it all.
what does it mean? how in heaven's name did we
get here? where the hell are we going? is it real? is
it actually happening? can it be that we're all just
passively watching? so empty, so bored inside, so
desperate to see a moment of truth, it never once
crosses our minds to do something.

NOVEMBER 21 AT 10:19 P.M.

scene opens on a young girl (red haired, pretty,
naturally waifish). she is with her parents in a den
that belongs in the museum of natural history. the
parents are seated on the paisleyed couch. they
look worried. their daughter, who has been acting
strange for the past week, has called this meeting

of the tribe. she has never done such a thing
before. instituted family discussion. so her parents
are understandably panic stricken. the girl asks
if anyone would like some water. she remembers
this question from family therapy way back when.
no one wanted water then and no one wants it
now. they want an end to the suspense. they want
their worst fears unconfirmed. so she tells them
everything she isnt. pregnant, infected with a killer
sex virus, addicted to drugs, expelled from school,
in a cult. the mother leans forward. her face is like
an oceanside community, sandbagged and boarded
up, bracing for high winds and floodwater. "you're
a lesbian," she says. "no, mom," the girl says, "i'm
not." and what if she was? would that be such a
catastrophe? but she needs to stay focused on the
real issue. she takes a deep breath. she looks at
the father. "remember," she says, "last summer?
remember the fourth of july?" tick-tock-tick-tock-
tick-tock. "well, i started writing to him," the girl
says. "i'm his pen pal."

the mother just stares at her. the girl cant read her
mind. never could. but the father. transparent as
a pane of glass. he's moved and sad and guilty and
swelling with fear. he knows what's coming next.
"i need your permission," his daughter says, "to
attend."

NOVEMBER 20 AT 5:55 P.M.

met Z this afternoon at venus body arts. did i
mention she decided to do it? she wanted me there,

wanted to be holding my hand at the moment of
pleasure-pain. she wanted also to be a war hero.
just give her a shot of whiskey and a bullet to bite
on. truth is, her voice was shaking, her hand was
shaking while she tried to smoke a cigarette on the
street. me? strange. how i didnt want any part of
it and did. how it made me sick and hungry at the
same time. i dont know why, but i wanted to see it.

in the back room, i watched her remove her pants,
then her undies. the piercer, a woman named eel
with a bone in her ear, slipped on some surgical
gloves. then Z laid back on the table. she looked so
helpless there. just lying there. waiting for the tip of
a needle. she's a girl, i almost said. she's just a girl.
but i didnt say anything. i just watched. the needle's
swift dart. the little ruby dewdrop before the blood
came. Z crying out, her hand tightening around
mine like maybe she was dying.

well, she lived. an hour later, i was waiting at the
bus stop with her. no biking for her. piercer's orders.
but soon. soon biking will be like a walk in the
clouds. "thanks, F," she said as the bus wheezed to a
stop. then she smiled. (oh, Z, dont you know you'll
never be ugly, no matter how hard you try?) once
she'd gone, i raced to the post office, rising off the
seat, pumping my legs until the muscles started to
burn. i ran up the steps and into the empty lobby.
fumbled for the gold key. the door squeaked open
and there it was. resting on an angle in the little
tunnel. i tore open the envelope. my breathing
echoed in the silent lobby and my eyes stung and

watered as i read his words. what am i going to do?
someone give me the answer. because he wants me
to be there. he wants me to watch him die.

NOVEMBER 12 AT 7:03 A.M.

a few points re: the talk in the chat room last nite.
1) you don't know him. all you know is the media
image of him. which is about as real as santa claus.
2) nothing is provable beyond a reasonable doubt in
the total ABSENCE of reason. 3) it was not a jury of
his peers. there wasn't one juror under the age of 21.
you do the math.

that being said, i want to be clear that i will not
tolerate hate chat on my site. if you dont have
anything nice to say, dont say any f***ing thing at
all.

NOVEMBER 11 AT 11:11 P.M.

i knew it as soon as he came home tonite. i knew
another one was going to happen. because he brings
it with him, the cold that has no freezing point, the
silence you can hear. his headlights sweeping thru
the windows, the car coughing in the driveway.
front door opens and closes. and then its in the
house with us. an evil spirit.

when i was younger, i would feel it but not
understand. that was back before i figured out what
he did sometimes at work, back when he was still
pure and lovable in my sight, and i thought our
bodies close together were more powerful than

anything. later i became afraid of him. phobic. i'd
hide like a cat. we all went to a shrink and we found
out it wasnt abnormal. an occupational hazard.
these days? these days i try to make believe i'm
ignorant. i try to remember what it was like to be a
little girl with so much of my mind like open prairie.
but i cant. you cant go back. only forward. and every
new day, you understand how blind you were the
day before. every day, more information collected.
more questions answered. less space to roam in.
what a fool you were. to not see it coming.

they're going to kill him. they're going to strap him
to a table and put him to sleep, like an animal.

NOVEMBER 1 AT 2:38 A.M.

as always on the first in frannyland, i have a new
color theme, new gallery photos, new archives.
november. the saddest month in my book. because
the colors of autumn are still fresh in your mind
and when you look at the trees you expect to see
beauty, you feel it should still be there. and its not.
its november. the trees are bare, the fallen leaves
are brittle and we crush them with our feet, we
burn them in our yards. and every day we feel whats
missing.

well, goodnite all. goodnite moon. goodnite dead
leaves. goodnite prison. goodnite my sweet.

OCTOBER 27 AT 10:01 A.M.

i've been thinking a lot about our chat of last
nite re: the boy (cue heartbeat). i admit, this

relationship isnt exactly traditional. but we're not interested in other people's idea of normal. yes, i appreciate your concern. i really do. i can see how, from your vantage point, the situation could look a little sketchy. but if you could just see his eyes. abandoned and hopeful. like pennies in a wishing well. if you could hold his hand and feel the bird-bone fingers. i'm telling you he could never use those hands for anything ungentle. there's been some kind of mistake. a nightmare error. because he loved her. he loved her so much it hurts me to think of it. and when he talks about her i feel ashamed of my heart. a jealous lump of muscle that just wants and wants and wants. its terrible, i know, there's something wrong with me, i know, but sometimes, sometimes i'm glad she's dead.

OCTOBER 12 AT 9:48 P.M.

big day in frannyland! slept over at Z's last nite, then this afternoon we biked into town. i was nervous and sweating the whole way. Z has two tattoos. a bracelet of thorns on her right arm, wrapping around her bicep and tricep. and a snake on her back, winding up the knobs of her spine. i wanted something colorful and (gasp!) a little less fiendish looking. to say my idea disappointed her would be an understatement. "F," she said, "that is so navel girl." "whatever," i said, "its what i want." tho' of course i couldn't tell her why.

i wish i didnt have to keep so much secret from Z. sometimes i feel like she doesnt know me at all, not half as well as you all do. i'm not sure why i dont tell her about the camera, why i cant confess to her the things i confess to you. i guess there are some things that are so private, you cant share them with people made of flesh.

so, can you guess where it is? feeling kinda shy at the moment, but later tonite i think. the unveiling. in the meantime, talk amongst yourselves. i'll just be in the bathroom admiring the lepidopteris adorabilis between the cups of my training bra. oops. me and my fat mouth.

ciao, franny

OCTOBER 2 AT 2:02 P.M.

was i talking in my sleep? i was dreaming. about her. you know. her. that SHE was the one on the screen, that it was HER site and HER domain. me and not me. when i spoke, the words came out of her mouth. so thats why i'm shaking. sitting here just staring at myself. its me on the screen, right? when i touch my cheek on the screen, i feel it. i can feel it. there seems to be something scientific about this, but what am i trying to prove?

SEPTEMBER 20 AT 3:58 A.M.

i saw him! we found a way and you'll just have to be satisfied knowing next to nothing about it. i know i said i'd never hide anything again, but this is different. dont you agree that there are times when promises have to be conditional? like when keeping them could threaten other people's jobs and hopes for pardon (or at the very least a commuted sentence)? i am sworn to secrecy and there's not a single soul who knows more than you do now. after all, who would i tell? Z? that'd be like throwing rocks at a hornets nest.

yours, franny

btw—he's every bit as sweet as i remember. every bit.

SEPTEMBER 3 AT 12:32 P.M.

first day of school. seventh grade. this year we learn how to put a condom on a banana.

i cant help but think about her. how it wouldve been her first day too. how it could be her sitting next to me in homeroom chewing on the end of a pencil, doodling in the margins of pop quizzes, in the bathroom mirror applying lip gloss, or in the next stall disposing of sanitary napkins. she was real and now she's dead. but what does that mean: real? and what does that mean: dead? how can death be real when i feel so alive? i think of him and i think of a butterfly emerging from its cocoon, testing its painted wings, then flying. free.

sent from my phone

AUGUST 24 AT 2:50 P.M.

oh, did i forget to mention he wrote me back? how absent minded of me. gosh, you all must be out of your minds with curiosity by now. BAD franny, BAD girl ;)

his letter. thats what i spent half the nite reading
in bed. and no that was not my book report i was
typing in the wee hours. i wrote to him all about
camp (well, not all. i left out the stuff about Z).
but i described the rest, all the things he cant see
hear feel experience himself. all month long, i
paid special attention. and you know what? there
IS some amazing stuff out there. sticky sap on
evergreen trees, owls asking questions in the night,
the feel of nite-black water on your naked body.
stars and stars and stars. there are still a few great
unwired spaces. but my god its so lonely to be out in
nowhereland without you all. after a while, staring
up at that nite sky, you begin to think like a tibetan
monk. if francesca cries out in the forest and no one
is there to see her, does she make a sound?

at those moments, i thought of him. and you want
to know something really weird? i imagined only he
could see me . . . and the sound i made was for him
alone. i imagined just the two of us. just him and
me forever in a place without cameras.

dont have a cow. i'm not going anywhere. i'm just
saying: i think i must be in love.

AUGUST 22 AT 10:53 P.M.

biked into town today with Z. sahara desert hot. by
the time we got there, her tank top was soaked thru.
kind of a sweathog, that Z. and not a big believer
in undergarments. she dismounted her motocross,
let it collapse onto the pavement, and leaned back
against a parked car. i got the impression i was

supposed to act aroused. i smiled a little and locked my ten-speed to a parking meter.

she's getting stranger and stranger. all month at camp she talked about masturbation and how girl love can save the world. one afternoon, we were walking together and found an old graveyard. i was kneeling down at some prehistoric stone and when i turned around she was bare chested backed up against a stone cross like somebody's savior. dont know why, but when i saw her like that i saw sasha. and i felt a shock in my stomach. i shouldnt have, i know, but i let her kiss me. on other days other things happened. and always, somehow, he was with us. Z couldnt see him, only i could. was there a spell out in the woods or fairy dust in the air? we've been back for a day and everythings a mess.

i finished locking my bike and helped hers up. she finally pushed off the car, looking hurt and angry and slutty. there were plenty of available parking meters, but she shoved her bike up against mine and chained the two of them together.

JULY 19 AT 5:20 P.M.

suddenly occurred to me the other day. is this going to remain my own private fantasy or am i going to act on it? you may wonder, what action could a girl possibly take in a situation like this? well i'll tell you.

she can bike into town and lease a post office box under an assumed name and slip the golden key onto her key ring. back at home, she can call the main switchboard and ask for a precise snail mail address. now she can start writing a letter. the hardest part. because what do you say to a boy like him, a boy who lives in another world you only half believe exists even though you can see it with your own eyes. she can write draft after draft until she gets it perfect. then she can fold it, mist it lightly with perfume, find an envelope and a postage stamp, and gasp out loud. her handwriting! she now must type the letter on her computer, print it, banish the unsaved document from existence, destroy the incriminating original in her father's shredder, create a label, seal the envelope.

the next time she is in town (which just might happen to be july 19) she can stand at a blue mailbox and hold the letter at the mouth of the dark chute. she can think about changing her mind. she can wonder if she's making a mistake. but in the end, though her body is hot and cold and trembling, she cant do anything but let it go.

love always, francesca

p.s. alas and alack, its that time of year when i must leave you and go into the wilderness for thirty days and thirty nites. i know this hurts. but remember. pain is the feeling of weakness leaving your body. a marine once told me that in a filthy chat room somewhere in the halls of montezuma. or was it the shores of tripoli?

i spent half the day today sitting on the tire swing just rocking, staring across the meadow at the walls. thinking about him. wondering. i could hear them in the exercise yard, their voices carrying out into the free world. like the dreamy buzz of bees in a hive. then suddenly i thought of something. something my father had mentioned one nite at dinner. i ran inside, up to the laptop. two keywords in the search engine. first hit on the list. i linked to the site and scrolled down, and when i found it, i thought, oh yes, F, you detective, you solver of puzzles!

SASHA PHILLIPS, D.O.C #997720
UNIT: DEATH ROW TIER: 13 CELL: 4

I AM A WHITE MALE, AGE 12½. MY INTERESTS
INCLUDE NUMISMATICS, BASEBALL, NATURE,
TIBETAN BUDDHISM. I AM AN AVID READER,
AND I KEEP A JOURNAL EVERY DAY. ALTHOUGH I
BELIEVE IN THE CYCLE OF DEATH AND REBIRTH,
SOMETIMES I STILL GET LONELY. IT'S HARD
BEING A BOY IN A MAN'S WORLD. SOME OF MY
FRIENDS SAY I AM TOO HONEST, BUT I THINK
IT WOULD BE WRONG TO NOT DISCLOSE THAT
I AM HERE FOR KILLING MY TWIN SISTER. I
DON'T REMEMBER DOING IT. BUT I REGRET IT
EVERY DAY. AND I HOPE TO SEE HER AGAIN ON
THE BARDO PLANE IN THE CLEAR LIGHT OF
DHARMA-KAYA, WHEN I CAN APOLOGIZE FOR
EVERYTHING I'VE FORGOTTEN. I AM LOOKING

FOR A FEMALE PEN PAL AROUND MY OWN AGE,
ANY RACE, COLOR, OR CREED. I MAY NOT HAVE
MUCH TIME LEFT, BUT I'VE LEARNED IN HERE
THAT SOMETIMES NO YEAR CAN BE AS LONG AS
A SINGLE DAY, AND THAT BROKEN LIVES CAN BE
MENDED, EVEN A MINUTE BEFORE MIDNIGHT.

i made sure, tonite, that one minute before the
stroke of twelve, i was standing by my window,
looking. at the sulfur bulb brightness, razor wire
glittering like tinsel, the shadow of a guard in one of
the gun towers. somewhere in the darkness at the
center of all that light, i thought, there's a boy. a boy
with brown eyes and dark hair, no older than me,
who did something terrible. god knows why.

JULY 1 AT 1:04 A.M.

a new month . . . time for new gallery pics, new
archives, a new color theme . . . and time, i've
decided, for a revision of the bio. i confess that all
these months i've been lying by omission. hiding
something. which just goes to show there ARE
things that cameras cant see. no, i'm not a lesbo
(tho' i'll try anything once). i'm a corrections brat.
my dad is the warden of a maximum-security prison
and we live about a stones throw away from the
perimeter.

he's not what you'd expect, my dad. he isnt
inhuman, like the ones in the movies. since he
took over here, things are a lot better than they
used to be. there are computers in the library. the
native americans have a sweat lodge. the elderly

can sometimes go home to die. last week, there was a family picnic, and he took me for an hour. food, games, music, even fireworks. before i left, he wanted me to meet one person in particular. a kid like me. at first, i thought he was someone's son or brother. but no. he lives there. he'll die there.

i'm not sure why i've kept this from you for so long. but now you know and i promise to never again conceal, censor, or otherwise obscure. you deserve to see all of me.

thunder now. lightning too. rain on the way. ok everyone, time for bed. tho' fyi i can't promise i'll be sleeping :) thank heaven for infrared night cams, right? keep your hands to yourself . . .

here comes the storm.

franny

GENERAL GRANT (2004–)

I never wanted a child. But it goes without saying that this is not why I gave in. To stand helplessly by while he walks out the door like this. I know where he got the stuff. He got it from Lecritz. And as soon as I deal with this situation, I intend to deal with that one. I will deal with that nutcase. Right now, I've got an emergency on my hands. My wife has already lost a breast. Now this. Is it all just for this? Are we put on this earth just to have things cut away from us, just to have things walk out the door and blow themselves up? I decide to try some reverse psychology.

"You know, we never wanted you."

"Oh, God, Malcolm. That is not true, Grant. Do not listen to him."

I press on. "No, it is."

"Sure, Dad."

"I'm not fucking kidding, Grant. You walk out the door like that and you're playing right into the irony of this situation."

"How ironic," he says.

She's been keeping her distance, trying to not touch him, afraid that a touch could drive him finally away and she'd feel forever after it was that touch, that moment of impulsiveness; but she does touch him now. Says: "We *always* wanted you, General."

For a moment, it seems that he's going to say good-bye, by closing his arms around his mother and pulling her tight against the four lumpy cylinders taped to his midriff, which do not look like real plastic explosives to me but more like mud masticated by wasps, as if stinging insects have been building on his body nests in the shape of plastic explosives and somehow we never noticed. But he doesn't hug her. The boy just stares at her, blinking, as if there's something in his eyes. A lash, a windblown molecule of glass. Me, he doesn't look at, period. Behind him, the front door is open. Steps lead down to the street. Last week's garbage on the curb. Still on the curb. Then he's striding past the two of us, back into the house.

"Now where are you going?" I say.

"I have to urinate first," he says. "Is that too ironic for you or something?"

We're frozen for a long moment as he disappears upstairs. To "his" bathroom. I listen to the creaking of the steps (the fifth step, the seventh—counting his steps for some reason), and the creaky steps make me think of the broken keys on an upright piano we once had, years ago, in the old house, in the basement. Grant took lessons for a year or two, then lost interest; then we sold the house and sold the piece of shit instrument for about a hundred dollars, and how hot and hollow my body feels now at the thought of all the pianos people give away and sell for nothing in life, all the piano lessons and the hours of practice, every song out of key, nothing ever *not* out of key, except for once in a great while, once in a while he'd get a whole measure right, in perfect tune, perfect time, and you'd hold your breath and discover yourself almost praying in the uncertain space between notes.

From upstairs, now: a flush; the sound of the running tap. The water runs and runs, and it hits me that he's stalling. For fifteen years, he has stalled and dawdled, put important and trivial things off, avoided commitments. Which is why it made no sense, the way he came downstairs a few minutes ago. But now I get it. I guarantee you he didn't have to take any piss in the first place.

"C'mon!" I shout.

"Malcolm?"

"Trust me," I tell my wife.

A couple more times I shout up there. I dare my boy to come down and see something through for once. I dare him to do it, just to make sure he won't. And sure enough he doesn't. The water is turned off, but the bathroom door never opens. The house slips into the silence of a forest between breezes. Silence, nothing—until finally you can hear something, barely. A sad bird calling from somewhere up above. My wife wants to go to him. She starts for the stairs. I hold her back. The kid may not be going anywhere, but he's still wired. As a parent, you have to know how to deal with situations. When to lay off and when to lean hard. Lecritz I will lean on. I will lean on that nutcase with every pound of weight in my body. But right now I just watch my wife go to the front door, close it and lock it; and as she turns around and makes an X with her arms over her reconstructed breasts, it comes to me without warning, the way repressed memories come back without warning, that one of the three of us will die before the others, and that will leave two.

BEREAVEMENT

His name was Rory. He'd been a late walker, a cautious boy who'd only recently taken his first steps when Mitch and Carolyn brought him to the lake in which he would drown. It still doesn't seem possible that he could've walked so far. Down the sloping lawn and across the full length of the dock. There have been moments when Mitch has doubted this version of events. He has actually contemplated the idea that one of his friends, or one of his friends' children, was somehow involved. This is how a cornered mind will lash out. If your baby can walk off the end of a dock and die in five feet of water, why couldn't one of your old college buddies be a monster, or the father of a monster? Thoughts like these provide a kind of relief. They function like a shunt, a metal tube driven into the skull to drain blood from the brain. Without them, the pressure would be too much.

He wants to try again.

Have another.

All along, Mitch has not wavered in his conviction that this is the best thing to do. The only thing. His wife doesn't agree. That's the worst part. Worse than the sadness and the guilt. It can feel at times like the entire world has been depopulated, like he and Carolyn are the only people left. Last two people on earth. Their course of action is clear. How can she *not* see this? She says: "You think we can re*place* him, Mitch? Even if we could—" But he's not talking about replacement, not in the sense that she is. She makes it sound like a pathetic delusion, like buying a set of bogus coins from a television shopping network. She makes it sound like betrayal.

"Not re*place*," he says.

"What then?"

He just looks at her. Glowers. Tries to express a distaste for her position so total it defies verbal communication. The truth is, he doesn't know what else to call it. He knows she's wrong, but can't prove the point.

"There's no word for it," he finally says.

"No word."

"In our language."

She pantomimes fatigue; presses two fingers to the bridge of her nose as if to control bleeding. "What language, then?"

"Please," he says, not sure exactly what he's asking for. Whatever it is, the answer will be no. No replacement, no reminder. No more risks.

Fine, he thinks.

He doesn't need her anyway. Mitch would like her to be involved, but he's not going to wait forever. He's waited too long already. A whole year lost. Summer again, and the cicadas are filling his head with dry dizzy noise. Soon, his friends will be gathering at the lake, as they do at this time every year. It's not that he doesn't talk to them anymore. Just that the better part of their daily lives—potty training, nursery school, tee ball—makes for cruel and unusual conversation; and when it comes to the accident, to concepts like chance and injustice, the members of his brilliant circle, the philosophy and history majors, seem out of their depth. Mitch has tried. He has tried to discuss the thing dispassionately. Over the phone, over drinks in the city. His friends respond as animals respond to a territorial incursion. It's not him they want to keep away, just his tragedy, which might be communicable somehow. Fine, he thinks. He doesn't need any of them. He can get over this, he can mend what's broken by himself. Without telling Carolyn, he goes ahead and orders the kit.

Normally, you take a saliva sample from the inside of the cheek, send the swab back to the lab by mail, and receive, four to six weeks later, what is known colloquially as the "fingerprint." Hair, especially absent the root, is less reliable and not guaranteed to provide a clean print; but he tries to be thankful they at least have this. An envelope full of it. A souvenir of Rory's first and only trip to the stylist. If only they'd frozen some skin cells or banked the umbilical cord blood, things would be a lot easier. But Mitchell and Carolyn didn't save anything like that. Mitch had never heard of a cord blood bank. His grasp of science (he had once been told at a cocktail party) was roughly equivalent to that of a yeoman farmer. Well, he'd never had a mind for it. In high school he'd barely passed biology, nearly failed chemistry, and weaseled his way out of physics. As an adult, he has chosen to ignore all these subjects, the way some people choose to ignore professional sports or the world of fashion. Carolyn's attitude is more actively hostile. She'll have no truck with science. When it came to childbirth, everything had to be natural. Having Rory was like starring in a reality television show about pioneer days. She delivered in the living room. No drugs for labor or pain, no doctors. Just a midwife, pots of hot water, and gore everywhere.

This is why he doesn't tell her about the kit. She would never understand. People's heads are full of myths and prejudice. Mitch himself doesn't fully understand. But he knows that what he is planning is no less pure, no less true than what happened in their living room that morning two years ago. Yes, you need a scientist to provide the code. But the code is not some artificial thing—it's not some pattern of lines on the side of a cereal box.

The code is *him*.

In a few weeks, the group will gather at the lake. Mitch figured the accident would end this yearly tradition, that his son's death would poison the place. No one would ever again want to assemble there in fraternity, mix drinks and barbeque steaks, play croquet, let their children on that dock, in that water. He figured they'd want to start over, somewhere free of guilt and ghosts.

He and Andrew discussed this a few weeks ago.

The two met at a quiet bar in the city and had one of those conversations that turned suddenly, needlessly defensive. But Andrew had started it by asking a strange question. Do you think you can ever go back to the house? Taken literally, the question didn't make much sense. The house belonged to Andrew's parents. Mitch knew them but couldn't envision any event (besides, heaven forbid, Andy's funeral) that would ever bring them all together again. Maybe his friend was speaking hypothetically, philosophically, the way he used to. Mitch thought of times spent high and drunk as an undergraduate: imagine you're married, you have a baby, and he drowns at my folks' house—could you ever go back?

"I could," Mitch responded. "Carolyn, I don't know."

Andrew nodded soberly, sipped his neat scotch. Then he said something about grieving, how people have different ways, different thresholds. He said he understood that this year might be too soon, but he hoped next summer. Everyone was hoping. Andy and Jamie, Rob and Jacqueline, Bryce and Lissa. The feeling was unanimous. That it won't be the same without Mitch and Carolyn.

"What won't?"

"You know, the lake."

Mitch was drinking mojitos. Though the day was not particularly hot, they were going down like Gatorade. He finished off his third while he tried to think of what to say. His head swam just a little.

"It just," he finally said, "seems so fucked up."

"What does?"

"Making plans. Like nothing happened."

Looking back, he can see how the words might be misinterpreted. But he'd meant no affront. He was simply amazed (he still is) by the persistence of life's patterns, how the world breathes in and out without pause, no matter how much death gets visited upon it. He didn't mean to single out his friends. He breathes, too—and how surprising it can be to hear his own breath! Like when he wakes up in the night to a darkness so total that even sound and feeling seem to have been disappeared. Then from somewhere inside the darkness, very close by but at a great distance, comes the sound of respiration. A man taking oxygen into his lungs just as he always has. Breathing. As if nothing has happened. In this way, he is no different from any other survivor.

Mitch has to admit, when the fingerprint arrives (he gets it at work, where he has directed all correspondence from the lab), it does sort of look like something that could be scanned at a cash register. For a few moments, to object doesn't seem unreasonable. He has the sense, as he stares at the card—which is about the size of a wallet-size photo and shows a series of black lines, unevenly spaced and varying in boldness—that he is looking at something he was never meant to see. Mitch is not a religious person. But just holding this image, this information, makes him feel like he's offending someone or something much more important than himself.

The phone rings. He ignores it. Rings again. This time he answers.

"It's me," Carolyn says.

"Hello, you."

There's a long silence. Mitch knows what it means. He knows he doesn't have to speak. Just be there. A year on, and these wordless pleas for help still come regularly. He holds the receiver firmly to his ear while he stares at their son's genetic code. All at once, the doubt is gone. Time to stop searching for a middle ground. His family needs him. Sometimes, in the midst of all the sadness and disagreement, he forgets that he used to be a father. Passing a fingertip over the pattern, he thinks he feels a gentle shock, a tendril of static electricity reaching out from it.

He'll have to go to the lake. The drive will take about four hours. He could finish his business and be back the same day, but it's easier to explain a longer absence. So he concocts a story about camping. He excavates the tent from the basement, finds a sleeping bag in an upstairs closet, conducts a search for citronella candles. "Have you seen the citronella?" he says, feeling like this authentic detail should put him above suspicion. Carolyn stands in the driveway, arms crossed, while he starts the car. She looks forlorn and unconvinced. Mitch pretends to remember the kerosene stove. "Now where is that damn thing?" he says, standing on a step stool in the garage, scanning shelves full of paint cans, motor oil, ceramic planters. He can feel her staring at him. He was in the clear, and he had to come back for the stove. "Look," she says, "are you having an affair?"

An affair.

Mitch isn't sure who he is anymore, but one thing he sure as hell *isn't* is a lover. That, more or less, is how he answers his wife's question. Then he says fuck the stove and leaves. As he steers his car through the mountains, everything seems yellowed, aged by the haze of midsummer. Himself included. An hour later, he stops to call her, to say he doesn't understand these surges of anger. It's not her he's angry with—he's just angry. She doesn't pick up of course (she screens every call, rarely picks up, and makes no exception for him), but this is okay. The answering machine has become a kind of mediator, not just recording words but refining communications, brokering peace.

How did they get here?

The path is clear, but he still can't square who they've become with who they were, who they were going to be. Granted, he and Carolyn don't go way back. Just four years, to Andrew's wedding. Best man and bridesmaid. As the mateless members of the wedding party, they felt almost duty bound to hook up, then after just a few hours started experiencing a sensation of kismet. They'd both crossed lately into their midthirties. They were tired of the singles scene; sick of renting, not owning; afraid to be out of step for very much longer. They both liked kids and wanted one. God, the falling happened fast—and the baby came so slow. Month after month, it refused to take root. Then it did, but not deeply enough. After the miscarriage was when he got worried. Mitch wanted to go for tests; Carolyn wouldn't. Just refused, flat out. She wanted everything to be natural and organic. No treatments, no test tubes, no technologies. In the end, that's how it happened. They had good old-fashioned sexual intercourse and life began inside her and a baby was born right in their home. See, she said while their hours-old son slept on her chest, I told you it'd work out.

Now, in a way, they're right back where they started. There are times (this is one of them: alone in the car, deep in a world of trees, no sound but air rushing through the open windows) when it seems fatherhood was just a dream he had; and losing his son, a nightmare within that dream; and waking life, nothing but a stasis, a waiting, the painfully slow process of reconstructing what you thought was real.

He pulls up to the house around two in the afternoon. There is no car in the drive, no one at home. He figured Andrew's parents would be here. A sunny weekend in July. He's come prepared with a bottle of Riesling, ready to have a nice visit before asking their permission to take what he needs. He doubts their property extends into the lake bed, but he doesn't want to offend. Now he doesn't have to worry. He'll do the thing and they'll never be the wiser, and he won't have to feign interest in the trends and tumults of Mrs. Levy's three separate book clubs. A deep breath. Mitch can see, beyond the house and past a few stately elms, the water. Bright as a mirror angled at the sun and the sky. He gets the spade and the box of heavy-duty freezer bags from the trunk. Starts for the shore. On the drive up, he hadn't been sure what to expect. How many times, in his dreams and daydreams, has he imagined the accident? Through the eyes of a god, through the eyes of his son. He's pictured the lake so many times. But to come back. To travel a great distance, to a place you've painted in the darkest of colors and see that it's still light, still bright blue and electric with sun glint. No evil, no killer to bring to justice. The water laps gently. Mitch removes his sandals, steps into the shallows. Minnows scatter. He sinks the spade into the bottom. Fills a plastic bag with wet earth. The substance is heavy and viscous, like fatty tissue. The more he digs, the more he gets on his skin and clothes. Finally, he just dispenses with the spade and uses his hands. As he works (packing bags, zipping them shut, and laying them on the dock), he glances at the house and the lake.
Fifteen years!

How many times that first summer alone (his major still unde-clared, a first great love stressing a fault line in his heart) did he run headlong over these wood planks, wet feet leaving short-lived prints, to plunge into this water, this very *same* water? Stoned, drunk, love struck. Croquet at dusk. Skinny-dipping. You scatter to different cities but always come back; and with each visit, the lake feels more like the most important place, the center, the heart of your own history. Significant others become spouses. Then, one summer, someone brings a baby. You still drink and smoke and screw, but the laws are changing a little. Is this the slippery slope everyone is always talking about? If you're the last, like Mitch, you start to feel out of place, like a kid brother tagging along on grown-up adventures, tripping on your untied shoelaces, falling behind. Is it inevitable that it happened, finally, right here? He remembers (it's a memory impressed on skin and nerves) walking Carolyn away from the tent and the music and the dancing, into the darkness, into a coolness that seemed to come from this water, the shore haloed with fireflies, everything wine-drunk, drunk on the promise of her.

"Mitchell?"

Shit, he thinks, looking up. Mrs. Levy has her arms crossed over her bosom; it's a vaguely compassionate posture. Mr. Levy, with whom Mitch has always had a shakier connection (ever since the time the older man discovered him, in the deep of the night, receiving oral sex in his favorite recliner), looks less sympathetic. He should shake his friend's father's hand, but his own is brown with mud. Mitch is knee-deep in their water. Twelve bags of silt are piled on their dock. His face is likely red from crying. "It's great to see you," he finally says. "I—I got you a Riesling."

It's one thing to gather the materials. Taking the next step, that's another matter entirely. Needless to say, Mitch has never done

anything like this before. He goes down to the basement apartment (unrented now for the better part of a year), and stares at
the eight pounds of mud stored in the refrigerator, and tries to
get up the nerve to lay it out on the counter and start shaping it.

What if he screws up?

He always has a hell of a time assembling things, even with
instructions; and he can't remember the last time he actually
made anything. Carolyn's the artsy one. She writes poetry and
once took a pottery class at the community college. Mitch is too
prosaic for this kind of undertaking. He writes legal briefs and
once had three training sessions at the gym.

They say the code is singular and infallible. It can mean only one
thing; it can produce only one outcome. Hydrogen and oxygen,
combined in a certain ratio, can only add up to water. Letters of
the alphabet arranged in a given order will always make the same
word. But water can be cold or warm, and a word can have more
than one meaning. Right? Mitch has no idea if such reasoning
is valid here. What's coldness or warmth but a feeling you get?
What the fuck is meaning? Days pass. The more he tries to work
out the questions, the less the answers seem to matter. Just bring
him back. It doesn't matter if he's perfect. He doesn't have to
be exactly the same. Every child has flaws. Every child changes.

Mitch reaches these conclusions on a Sunday night (sitting up
in bed, viewing but not comprehending the football game) and
decides he will do it in the morning. He'll take a sick day. Start
first thing, right after Carolyn leaves the house. He always feels
fresh, most alert and creative, in the morning.

"Andrew called before."

"Who?"

"Andy. Levy."

The television is dark. His wife reads beside him by the light
of a low-wattage bulb, not taking her eyes off the page as she

speaks. He must've fallen asleep. Andrew. Mitch has been waiting for this call, dreading it, hoping his friend would exercise the
better part of valor and keep his mouth shut if tempted to open
it. Now Mitch shuffles into the bathroom, cleans his teeth. As
he does whenever his wife is in earshot, he sits to urinate. In the
last year, their marriage has been defined by this kind of timid-
ity. They burn incense to mask odors. Dress for bed like people
from another era. It's the middle of summer, and they both wear
pajamas, tops and bottoms. When he climbs back in bed, he lies
on his side, facing away from her and the light. Finally, she says:
"He said you were out at the lake."

"I was."

"Doing what?"

He considers telling her everything. Thinks about asking, honestly, for her help. He could turn to her, look into her eyes. Maybe
if they looked at each other, really tried to see, instead of always
angling their heads away. But he can't make himself move.

"You didn't have to lie about it," she says softly.

"I didn't lie."

"Hide it then. Look, Mitch. We've both got our ways. There's
nothing wrong with that. I just can't do it your way." He can hear
her turn down the page of her book and close the cover. "It's
like—it's like you want to make grief part of your daily life. Set
a place at the table for him every night and just let it be empty."

"Not empty."

"No, I know. Not empty."

"I'd like to know what's so strange about that. You act like it's
crazy to want him back." He shuts his eyes, hard. "Don't you want
to be a mother again?"

There's no answer. He's not expecting one. The question has
come to be rhetorical; and though he always asks it in a tone of
honest inquiry, he knows deep down that his motives are egoistic.

He doesn't know how else to change her mind, except through an appeal to her own self-interests. Because he hasn't believed for a moment this past year that she doesn't want their son back, wouldn't take him back if given the chance, or if forced into it. She's depressed. It's so obvious. But she refuses to treat this pain of letting go, the same way she refused to treat the pain of bringing him into the world—and as for the remedies of physical love, she's so frightened of getting pregnant again, she won't let her own husband finish inside her. So what is he supposed to do? What options does she leave him?

"It's like a maze," she says.

"What?"

"It's like a maze we keep getting lost in. You would think two grown people could learn their way through it."

He rolls over to face her, finds her staring down at him. It's an unnerving moment. He's not sure if it's the light or her posture, but she seems to be regarding him from a great distance and with a terrible intent. It's as if, while he was turned away, she ran from him and is poised now to slip completely out of sight. It *is* a maze, he thinks—if he doesn't act, if something doesn't change, she will disappear into its inscrutable design and they'll spend the rest of their lives searching separately for the exit.

In the morning, he sits at the patio table on the back deck while she gets ready for work. Beyond the wooded interior of their city block, there are the monolithic buildings of the capitol plaza, which stand over them always, watchful and all seeing; and closer by, on the fences that divide the backyards and gardens, the neighborhood cats, four of them, who also seem to be looking at him, judging him dispassionately. He is drinking strong coffee, waiting for the sun, getting that feeling again, the one he had in the office the day the fingerprint arrived. Mitch knows he has every right to possess the code. After all, he's the father, and half of it came from him. Still. He can't completely rid himself of a fear he's known, up to now, only in dreams. He can't figure it out. He can't see why what he's about to do should scare him in this way, the way he's scared when he dreams of having blood on his hands—but he can't deny the correlation. As if this, too, is a thing you do in passion and immediately regret, a thing you know not to do and can never undo once you've done it. He holds the coffee mug and stares at his hands. The first light, feeling its way through the leaves, finds every fine hair on his fingers, every crease on his knuckles, all the dirt under his bitten nails. From the street, the pounding heartbeat of rap music on a car stereo; from a nearby open window, the sound of a baby crying out in vain. When Carolyn touches his shoulder, he jumps as if at a gunshot, overturns the mug. "Sorry," she says. "Just wanted you to know, I'm leaving."

◊

Only after speaking these words does she see the double meaning. She didn't mean it that way, didn't mean to mean two things at once. But as she walks through the house then down the front steps to the street, trying to remember where the car is parked, she can't say that both meanings aren't true. She scans the block. No sign of her little hybrid. She is fed up with this shit. She wants parking. She wants the stupid city to issue resident permits; she wants a driveway; she wants a world without cars. She doesn't know what she wants. Left, she recalls. Halfway down Hudson. She remembers now; she got home late from the board meeting last night and had to park near the plaza, near the underground garage, in a violet light more unnerving than total darkness for the way it turns night into a stage where something seems bound to happen. Since the accident, she's been unable to decide. Is she immune to danger or does she carry it inside her like a pathogen? Nothing bad has happened in the past year, though it seems at every moment that something will. A highway crash that will put her in a coma, for example; or a tragedy much greater, some dark premeditated thing, touching her and countless others at the same time. Today, the anxiety is just about her, centered in her body. In her uterus, to be exact. If asked to explain herself, she wouldn't be able to. She just feels different there. Different than she felt yesterday. But she *knows* this feeling, this sensation that isn't really happening yet, this foreshadow of a feeling.

Not possible.

She's been taking birth control pills for months. Her ovaries are not releasing eggs. Her body, artificially flooded by hormones, thinks it's pregnant all the time. Even if her body is the one in ten thousand that can figure out the trick, it's been a long time since there's been any semen inside her. Still, the feeling is so singular. Once you feel it, you will never mistake it for anything else. The joyful terror of something beginning, of a life-to-be, of life that is not yet living. No one knows, but this has happened before. Twice. Two times since the accident, she has sworn she was pregnant—and not without reason. Nausea in the morning; sudden storms of sadness forming over her heart; physical changes that are just uncanny. When she finally reaches the car (right where she left it, but wedged now between two sport utility vehicles), she starts the engine, turns up the air, then eases a hand inside her blouse and touches her breast. God, it aches. They've both swelled up overnight, just like the last time, and her nipples are secreting a milky fluid. She remembers reading about this in a baby book. The medical term escapes her, but the facts of the condition (a desire for, or a fear of, a baby so intense that the mind and body both come to believe it's there) are unforgettably bizarre. There's something wrong with her. Really wrong. She's not getting better—she's getting worse.

When Carolyn returns at dusk, she encounters the usual scene. The neighborhood children running up and down the sidewalk, weaving among the parked cars, chasing each other into the street. Tonight she finds a spot near the house, in the heart of all this dangerous play. As she backs in (one of the boys darting behind her, drumming his hands on the trunk of the car), she makes eye contact through the passenger window with one of the girls, who immediately looks away, runs away. Carolyn knows her, or knew her. A year ago—when Carolyn was a mother, a blond mother pushing her blond infant in a stroller—you might have called them friends. For all the girls on the block, Carolyn had held a strange fascination. They flocked around her like disciples, called her name whenever she appeared on the sidewalk, inquired in reverent tones about the baby. Now, sometimes they will wave sheepishly; but just as often they will avoid her, as if a parent has told them to. She kills the motor. Sits listening to the squealing and the laughter, which will go on until well after dark, then unclicks her seat belt. Exits the car. Locks it by key-chain remote control as she crosses the street. Can't stop herself, as she climbs the stairs of the house and opens the door, from looking back to see if any of the children are watching her. They're not. They're in their own world, playing in the street, attracting tragedy. It's a miracle they're all still alive.

Inside, she is surprised to hear the sound of the television and to find her husband in the back room, wearing jeans, holding a drink in his hand.

"You're home early," she says.

He nods.

"Everything okay?"

"Sure, why?"

She shakes her head. "Good day?"

"Okay," he says. "Fine. The usual, you know. A day, like any other day."

For the rest of the evening, he drinks expensive scotch and gives off the aura of a bad liar. Nothing's wrong, he says. Office politics. But she's certain he never went to work today. How many days like this have there been? If only it were an affair, something as trivial as sex. But there's a different kind of secret inside him, as disturbing as the one she is keeping from him even now. Upstairs, she closes herself in the bathroom and removes the home test from its box. Urinates on the stick and waits. Negative, of course. What more proof does she need? Yet the hallucination will not fade. She needs to talk to someone. She has friends, of course; but none of them will understand. They're all mothers, all with living, breathing children. Carolyn has nothing in common with them anymore. They say they can't imagine what she goes through. This is true. It's like trying to imagine what lies beyond the edges of the universe. Try again, they say. So earnest and innocent. Like it's a simple matter of calling for a stork. As for Mitch. How could she reveal this to him—that she has waking dreams about the very thing he wants so badly? She looks again at the stick. Negative. She should feel nothing but relief. You can't know what she knows and want to go through it all again. What if she lost another? What if one died inside her? After months, weeks, days. It doesn't matter when life begins. It doesn't matter if it's nothing but a clump of cells, doesn't matter what it is or isn't. This isn't about science—it's about loss.

Late that night (she knows without looking at the clock that it's late because the bedroom is dark, meaning the floodlights have been switched off at the base of the monolithic buildings of the plaza), she seems to hear her dead son crying. Her blood catches fire. All at once, awake. Already propped up on one elbow. Listening. Mitch not in the bed, not in the room. The air coming through the open windows, stirring the gauzy curtains, is cool enough to make her shiver. Maybe a cat in heat, maybe a neighbor's baby, maybe just her imagination. Because nothing now. No sound at all. It's a summer night, she thinks. Regardless of the hour, there should be noise. Traffic, music, a quarrel in the street. Yet it's unnaturally quiet; and something about this silence, the way it wiped out those familiar cries, makes her eyes hurt. She gets up, walks out to the landing at the top of the stairs, where one of the wooden banister still shows, in the form of several small holes, the evidence of the safety gate that was once affixed there. From here, she can see the front door (closed, its curtained window glowing with light from the nearby streetlamp), and she can hear the workings of the antique sunburst clock that hangs on the wall over the sofa. That's all. No other light or sound. Wherever her husband may be, he must be motionless in the dark. Passed out, she guesses, on the sofa below the clock; or still drinking, soundlessly, on the back porch. Time goes by, the way a river goes by when you stand on its bank—with a speed that's impossible to perceive until something, some floating object, ends the illusion of stillness.

There it is!

Not a cat, not someone else's baby, not a trick of the mind. This cry is louder and realer than the last, and seems to come from downstairs.

She does not want to go down there. This panic, this tearfulness. Same as that day at the lake. The same sense that something is happening that cannot possibly be happening. He can't be dead; he can't be alive. Carolyn tries to say his name. Cannot. Her voice is being seized in her throat. So scared, but she puts a hand on the smooth wooden rail and moves closer. She moves through the first floor of the house, switching on lights, searching for him, worrying that she's too late. That he's been crying for a long time and she failed to hear him. Even a few moments are too many. Just a few moments of unconsciousness, of self-centeredness. You can't look away. Never look away. Because it only takes moments for little feet to reach the end of solid wood planking and step off into the nothing of water. She can't find him anywhere. Almost every light in the house shining. But does she expect this light to make seeing easier? She turns them all off and stands in the darkness, breathing, trying to breathe. That's when things come clear. Not just a cry this time. A word. Two distinct syllables spoken from below her, from under the wooden floor.

Mama.

She doesn't even think about keys, just goes out to the porch into the night, then down the steps that lead to the yard. They have let it go. The area is thick with flowering weeds, which have choked the last tenant's perennials to death and given the little stone fairy (goddess of the garden, left behind on moving day) the air of a ruin. The apartment is faintly lit. The window blinds are drawn, but there's another window in the door; and when she looks through, she is unsure of what she's seeing. Two figures. One a man; the other not a ghost, not a shining spirit. No, whatever her husband is holding in his arms is made of solid matter. It's a baby and it isn't. It's her son and it isn't. If there weren't movement, mouth making noise and arms reaching into space, she wouldn't think him to be living; if they'd buried a body instead of scattering ash, she might think her husband had been to the grave with a shovel. Grayish flesh, the color of unfired clay; features that are familiar but distorted and make her think not of a twin but of a brother afflicted with some kind of chromosomal disorder. This is the terror she never wanted to feel again. He looks sick, like maybe he might not live, maybe not even until morning. But she's not too late! She's not too late this time!

Carolyn lifts her hand and raps on the glass and meets her husband's eyes, and becomes aware of an anger, fiery hot but so deep within her she can't actually feel it, she just knows it's there. How could he do this to her? Someday, the question will find a way to the surface; or it might burn out of sight and out of reach forever. The baby could live. They are at the door now, father and son. She can see the baby much more clearly, and she is questioning her first impression. His flesh looks warm with blood; his defects, nothing more than a trick of dim light. The lock clicks open, the doorknob turns, the door moves on its hinges. Then he's in her arms. There is a disconcerting odor of natural decay, like wet fallen leaves or soft fallen fruit, but he's breathing, he's breathing. "Rory," she says, choking out the name, crying as she hasn't done in so very long. Not since that day at the lake. An outburst that seems to come not from her but *through* her, as if she is channeling the sadness of someone else, as if there are emotions always struggling to make themselves heard from the other side—massing, crushing against the barrier that divides here from there—finding in people like her an opening.